The Paternity Promise

MERLINE LOVELACE

MILLS & BOON

First published in Great Britain 2012
by Mills & Boon, an imprint of Harlequin (UK) Limited.
Large Print edition 2012
Harlequin (UK) Limited,
Eton House, 18-24 Paradise Road,
Richmond, Surrey TW9 1SR

© Merline Lovelace 2012

ISBN: 978 0 263 22983 7

Harlequin (UK) policy is to use papers that are natural,
renewable and recyclable products and made from
wood grown in sustainable forests. The logging
and manufacturing process conform to the legal
environmental regulations of the country of origin.

Printed and bound in Great Britain
by CPI Antony Rowe, Chippenham, Wiltshire

Dear Reader,

When my husband and I spent a week in the small town of Saint-Rémy-de-Provence in the south of France, we absolutely fell in love with the place. And since I'm always on the lookout for exciting locales for books, I knew Saint-Rémy would eventually show up in one.

I didn't, however, expect the road that led my characters there would be so bumpy and pitted with tension, sexual and otherwise. I had great fun overcoming the roadblocks with Grace and Blake—hope you do, too!

All my best, and happy reading,

Merline Lovelace

"You Want Me To Come Back As Molly's Nanny?"

"Not as her nanny," Blake replied. "As my wife."

He could certainly understand Grace's slack-jawed astonishment. She'd wormed her way into his life and Molly's heart. She'd lied to him. Yet the hole she'd left behind had grown deeper with each hour she was gone.

Molly's unexpected arrival had already turned his calm, comfortable routine upside down. This doe-eyed blonde had kicked it all to hell. So he felt a savage satisfaction to see his chaotic feelings mirrored on her face.

"You're crazy! I can't marry you!"

"Why not?"

"Because...because... What about love, Blake? And...sex?"

With a smooth move, he pushed himself off the sofa. Grace wasn't prepared when he stopped mere inches away. With him standing so close, her chest rose and fell with every breath.

"That's not a problem, Grace. The sex is definitely doable."

MERLINE LOVELACE

A career Air Force officer, Merline Lovelace served at bases all over the world. When she hung up her uniform for the last time she decided to combine her love of adventure with a flair for storytelling, basing many of her tales on her own experiences in uniform. Since then she's produced more than ninety action-packed sizzlers, many of which have made the *USA TODAY* and Waldenbooks bestseller lists. Over eleven million copies of her books are available in some thirty countries.

When she's not tied to her keyboard, Merline enjoys reading, chasing little white balls around the fairways of Oklahoma and traveling to new and exotic locales with her handsome husband, Al. Check her website at www.merlinelovelace.com or friend her on Facebook for news and information about her latest releases.

To the Elite Eight, and the
wonderful times we've shared.
Thanks for giving me such
terrific fodder for my books!

One

His fists balled inside the pockets of his tuxedo pants, Blake Dalton forced a smile as he stood amid the wedding guests jamming the black-and-white-tiled foyer of his mother's Oklahoma City mansion. The lavish reception was finally winding down. The newlyweds had just paused in their descent of the foyer's circular marble staircase so the bride could toss her bouquet. The couple were mere moments from departing for their honeymoon in Tuscany.

Blake was damned if he'd block their escape. His twin had waged a tumultuous battle to win the stubbornly independent pilot he'd finally finessed to the altar. Alex had earned these two weeks in Tuscany with his new bride, away from his heavy responsibilities as CEO of Dalton International.

Blake had no problem taking up the slack in his absence. An MBA, a law degree and almost a decade of handling the corporation's complex legal affairs had honed the leadership and managerial skills he'd developed as DI's CFO. He and Alex regularly took over sole control of the multibillion-dollar conglomerate during each other's frequent business trips.

No, the job wasn't the problem.

Nor was it their mother, who'd waged a fierce and unrelenting campaign to get her sons married and settled down for over a year now.

Blake's glance cut to the matriarch of the Dalton clan. Her hair was still jet-black, with only a hint of silver at the temples. She wore a melon-colored Dior lace dress and an expression of smug satisfaction as she surveyed the newly married couple. Blake knew exactly what she was thinking. One son down, one to go.

But it was the baby peering over his mother's

shoulder that made his fist bunch even tighter and his heart squeeze inside his chest. In the weeks since person or persons unknown had left the six-month-old on his mother's doorstep, Molly had become as essential to Blake as breathing.

DNA testing had proved with 99.99 percent certainty that the bright-eyed infant girl was a Dalton. Unfortunately, the tests hadn't returned the same accuracy as to *which* of the Dalton brothers had fathered the baby. Although even identical twins carried distinctive DNA, there were enough similarities to fog the question of paternity. The report had indicated a seventy-seven percent probability that Alex was the father, but the issue couldn't be completely resolved until the lab matched the father's DNA with that of the mother.

As a result, the Dalton brothers had spent several uncomfortable weeks after Molly's arrival tracking down the women they'd connected with early last year. Alex's list had been considerably longer than Blake's, but none of the potential candidates—including the woman who'd just become Ms. Alex Dalton—had proved to be the baby's mother. Or so they'd thought.

A noisy round of farewells wrenched Blake's gaze from the baby. He looked up to find his brother searching the crowd. It was like looking in a mirror. Both he and Alex had their father's build. Like Big Jake Dalton, they carried six feet plus of solid muscle. They'd also inherited their father's electric blue eyes and tawny hair that the hot Oklahoma sun streaked to a dozen different shades of gold.

Blake caught Alex's eye and casually, so casually, shook his head. He had to forcibly blank both his face and his mind to block any more subtle signals. In the way of all twins, the Dalton brothers could pick up instantly on each other's vibes. Time enough for Alex and Julie to hear the news when they got back from Tuscany. By then Blake would have dealt with it. And with the shock and fury it had generated.

He rigidly suppressed both emotions until the newlyweds were on the way to the airport. Even then he did his duty and mingled until the last guests finally departed. His training as an attorney stood him in good stead. No one, not even his mother, suspected there was fury boiling in his gut.

"Whew!" Ebullient but drooping, Delilah Dalton kicked off her heels. "That was fun, but I'm glad it's over. Went off well, don't you think?"

"Very," Blake answered evenly.

"I'm going to check on Molly." She swooped up her shoes and padded on stockinged feet to the circular marble staircase. "Then I'm hitting the tub to soak for an hour. You staying here tonight?"

"No, I'll go back to my place." With a vicious exercise of will, he kept his voice calm. "Would you ask Grace to come down? I'd like to talk to her before I go."

His mother lifted a brow at his request to speak to the woman she'd hired to act as a temporary nanny. In the weeks since a baby had dropped into the lives of all three Daltons, Grace Templeton had proved indispensable. Become almost part of the family. So much so that she'd served as

Julie's maid of honor while Blake stood up with Alex as best man.

She'd also started the wheels turning in Delilah's fertile mind. His mother had begun dropping unsubtle hints in recent days about how sweet Grace was. How well she interacted with Molly. And just tonight, how good Blake had looked standing beside her at the altar. The fact that he'd begun to think along those same lines only added to the fury simmering hot and heavy.

"Tell Grace I'll be in the library."

For once Delilah was too tired to pry. She merely waved her shoes and continued up the stairs. "Will do. Just don't keep her too long. She has to feel as whipped as I do."

She was about to feel a whole lot more whipped. Yanking on the ends of his black bow tie, Blake stalked down the hall to the oak-paneled library. The soft glow from the recessed lighting contrasted starkly with his black mood as he retrieved the report he'd stuffed into his pocket more than an hour ago. The facts were no less shattering now than they had been then. He was still trying to absorb their impact when Grace Templeton entered the library.

"Hey, Blake. Delilah said you wanted to talk to me."

His eyes narrowed on the slender blonde, seeing her in a wholly different light. She'd changed from the lilac, off-the-shoulder tea gown she'd worn for the wedding. She'd also released her pale, almost silvery hair from its sophisticated upsweep. The ends now brushed the shoulders of a sleeveless white blouse sporting several large splotches.

"'Scuze the wet spots," she said, brushing a hand down her front with a rueful laugh in her warm brown eyes. "Molly got a little lively during her bath."

Blake didn't respond. He merely stood with his shoulders rigid under his tux as she hitched a hip on the wide, rolled arm of the library's sofa.

"What did you want to talk about?"

Only then did she pick up on his silence. Or maybe it was his stance. Her head tilting, she gave him a puzzled half smile.

"Something wrong?"

He countered her question with one of his own. "Did you happen to notice the man who arrived at the reception just before Alex and Julie left?"

"The guy in the brown suit?" She nodded slowly, still trying to gauge his odd mood. "I saw him, and couldn't help wondering who he was. He looked so out of place among the other guests."

"His name's Del Jamison."

Her brow creased. Blake guessed she was mentally sorting through the host of people she'd met during her stint as Molly's temporary nanny. When she drew a blank, he supplied the details.

"Jamison's a private investigator. The one Alex and I hired to help search for Molly's mother."

She was good, he thought savagely. Very good. Her cinnamon eyes transmitted only a flicker of wariness, quickly suppressed, but she couldn't keep the color from leaching out of her cheeks. The sudden pallor gave him a vicious satisfaction.

"Oh, right." The shrug was an obvious attempt at nonchalance. "He was down in South

America, wasn't he? Checking the places where Julie worked last year?"

"He was, but after Julie made it clear she wasn't Molly's mother, Jamison decided to check another lead. In California."

She couldn't hide her fear now. It was there in the quick hitch in her breath, the sudden stillness.

"California?"

"I'll summarize his report for you." Blake used his courtroom voice. The one he employed when he wanted to drive home a point. Cool, flat, utterly devoid of emotion. "Jamison discovered the woman I was told had died in a fiery bus crash was not, in fact, even on that bus. She didn't die until almost a year later."

The same woman he'd had a brief affair with. The woman who'd disappeared from his life with no goodbye, no note, no explanation of any kind. Aided and abetted, he now knew, by this brown-eyed, soft-spoken schemer who'd wormed her way into his mother's home.

And into Blake's consciousness, dammit. Every level of it. As disgusted by her duplicity as by the hunger she'd begun to stir in him, he stalked across the room. She sprang to her feet at his approach and tried to brazen it out.

"I don't see what that has to do with me."

Still he didn't lose control. But his muscles quivered with the effort of keeping his hands off her.

"According to Jamison, this woman gave birth to a baby girl just weeks before she died."

His baby! His Molly!

"She also had a friend who showed up at the hospital mere hours before her death." He planted his fists on the sofa arm, boxing her in, forcing her to lean back. "A *friend* with pale blond hair."

"Blake!" The gold-flecked brown eyes he'd begun to imagine turning liquid with desire widened in alarm. "Listen to me!"

"No, Grace—if that's really your name." His temper slipped through, adding a whiplash to his voice. "You listen, and listen good. I don't know how much you figured you could extort from our family, but the game ends now."

"It's not a game," she gasped, bent at an awkward angle.

"No?"

"No! I don't want your money!"

"What do you want?"

"Just… Just…!" She slapped her palms against his shirtfront. "Oh, for Pete's sake! Get off me."

He didn't budge. "Just what?"

"Dammit!" Goaded, she bunched a fist and pounded his chest. Her fear was gone. Fury now burned in her cheeks. "All I wanted, all I cared about, was making sure Molly had a good home!"

Slowly, Blake straightened. Just as slowly, he moved back a step and allowed her only enough space to push upright. Slapping a rigid lid on his anger, he folded his arms and locked his gaze on her face. Assessing. Considering. Evaluating.

"Let's start at the beginning. Who the hell are you?"

Grace balanced precariously on the sofa arm, her thoughts chaotic. After all she'd been through! So much fear and heartache. Now this? Just when she'd started to breathe easy for the first time in months. Just when she'd thought she and this man might…

"Who are you?"

He repeated the question in what she'd come to think of as his counselor's voice. She'd known Blake Dalton for almost two months now. In that time she'd learned to appreciate his even temperament. She admired even more his ability to smoothly, calmly arbitrate between his more outspoken twin and their equally strong-willed mother.

Oh, God! Delilah!

Grace cringed inside at the idea of divulging even part of the sordid truth to the woman who'd become as much of a friend as an employer. Sick at the thought, she lifted her chin and met Blake's cold, unwavering stare.

"I'm exactly who I claim to be. My name *is* Grace Templeton. I teach…I taught," she corrected, her throat tight, "junior high social studies in San Antonio until a few months ago."

She paused, trying not to think of the life she'd put on hold, forcing herself to blank out the image of the young teens she took such joy in teaching.

"Until a few months ago," Blake repeated in the heavy silence, "when you asked for an extended leave of absence to take care of a sick relative.

That's the story you gave us, isn't it? And the principal of your school?"

She knew they'd checked her out. Neither Delilah nor her sons would allow a stranger near the baby unless they'd vetted her. But Grace had become so adept these past years at weaving just enough truth in with the lies that she'd passed their screening.

"It wasn't a story."

Dalton's breath hissed out. Those sexy blue eyes that had begun to smile at her with something more than friendliness the past few weeks were now lethal.

"You and Anne Jordan were related?"

Anne Jordan. Emma Lang. Janet Blair. So many aliases. So many frantic phone calls and desperate escapes. Grace could hardly keep them straight anymore.

"Anne was my cousin."

That innocuous label didn't begin to describe Grace's relationship to the girl who'd grown up just a block away. They were far closer than cousins. They were best friends who'd played dolls and whispered secrets and shared every event in their young lives, big and small.

"Were you with her when she died?"

The question came at her as swiftly and mercilessly as a stiletto aimed for the heart. "Yes," she whispered, "I was with her."

"And the baby? Molly?"

"She's your daughter. Yours and…and Anne's."

Blake turned away, and Grace could only stare at the broad shoulders still encased in his tux. She ached to tell him she was sorry for all the lies and deception. Except the lies had been necessary, and the deception wasn't hers to tell.

"Anne called me," she said instead. "Told me she'd picked up a vicious infection. Begged me to come. I jumped a plane that same afternoon but when I got there, she was already slipping into a coma. She died that evening."

Blake angled back to face her. His eyes burned with an unspoken question. Grace answered this one as honestly as she could.

"Anne didn't name you as Molly's father. She was almost out of it from the drugs they'd pumped into her. She was barely coherent… All

I understood was the name Dalton. I knew she'd worked here, so…so…"

She broke off, her throat raw with the memory.

"So you brought Molly to Oklahoma City," Blake finished, spacing every word with frightening deliberation, "and left her on my mother's doorstep. Then you called Delilah and said you'd just happened to hear she needed a temporary nanny."

"Which she did!"

He gave that feeble response the disgust it deserved. "Did you enjoy watching my brother and me jump through hoops trying to determine which of us was Molly's father?"

"I told you! I didn't know which of you it was. Not until I'd spent some time with you."

Even then she hadn't been sure. The Dalton twins shared more than razor-sharp intelligence and devastating good looks. Grace could see how her cousin might have succumbed to Alex's charisma and self-confidence. She'd actually figured him for Molly's father until she'd come to appreciate the rock-solid strength in quiet, coolly competent Blake.

Unfortunately, Blake's self-contained personality had made her task so much more difficult. Although friendly and easygoing, he kept his thoughts to himself and his private life private. If he'd had a brief affair with a woman who'd worked for him, only he—and possibly his twin—had known about it.

Grace had hoped the DNA tests they'd run would settle the question of Molly's paternity. She'd been as frustrated as the Dalton brothers at the ambiguous results.

Then they'd launched a determined search for Molly's mother and thrown Grace in a state of near panic. She'd sworn to keep her cousin's secret. She had no choice but to do just that. Molly's future depended on it. Now Blake had unearthed at least a part of that secret. She couldn't tell him the rest, but she could offer a tentative solution.

"As I understand it, Molly's parentage can't be absolutely established unless the father's DNA is matched with the mother's. She…Anne…was cremated. I don't have anything of hers to give you that would provide a sample."

Not a hairbrush or a lipstick or even a postcard

with a stamp on it for Molly to cling to as a keep-sake. The baby's mother had lived in fear for so long. She'd died the same way, mustering only enough strength at the end to extract a promise from her cousin to keep Molly safe.

"You could test my DNA," Grace said, determined to hold to that promise. "I've read that mitochondria are inherited exclusively through the female line."

She'd done more than read. She'd hunched in front of the computer for hours when not tending to Molly. Her head had spun trying to decipher scientific articles laced with terms like hypervariable control regions and HVR1 base pairs. It had taken some serious slogging, but she'd finally come away with the knowledge that those four-hundred-and-forty-four base pairs determined maternal lineage. As such, they could theoretically be used to trace a human's lineage all the way back to the mitochondrial Eve. The Daltons didn't need to go that far back to confirm Molly's heritage. They just needed to hop over one branch on her family tree.

The same thought had obviously occurred to

Blake. His eyes were chips of blue ice as he delivered an ultimatum.

"Damn straight you'll give me a DNA sample. And until the results come back, you'll stay away from Molly."

"What?"

"You heard me. I want you out of this house. Now."

"You're kidding!"

She discovered an instant later that he wasn't. In two strides he'd closed the distance between them and wrapped his fist around her upper arm. One swift tug had her off the sofa arm and marching toward the library's door.

"Blake, for God's sake!" As surprised as she was angry, she fought his grip. "I've been taking care of Molly for weeks now. You can't seriously think I would do anything to hurt her."

"What I think," he returned in a voice as icy as his eyes, "is that there are a helluva lot of holes in your story. Until they're filled in, I want you where I can watch you day *and* night."

Two

"Get in."

Blake held open the passenger door of his two-seater Mercedes convertible. The heat of the muggy July evening wrapped around them, almost as smothering as the worry and fear that clogged Grace's throat.

"Where are we going?"

"Downtown."

"I need to tell Delilah that I'm leaving," she protested. "Get some of my things."

"I'll let my mother know what's happening. Right now all you need to do is plant your behind in that seat."

If Grace hadn't been so stunned by this un-expected turn of events, the brusque command might have made her blink. This was Blake. The kind, polite, always solicitous Dalton twin. In the weeks since she'd insinuated herself into Delilah's home, she'd never known him to be anything but patient with his sometimes over-bearing mother, considerate with the servants and incredibly, achingly gentle with Molly.

"Get in."

She got. Even this late in the evening, the pale gray leather was warm and sticky from the July heat. The seat belt cracked like a rifle shot when she clicked it into place.

As the convertible rolled down the curved driveway, Grace fought to untangle her nerves. God knew she should be used to having her life turned upside down without warning. It had hap-pened often enough in the past few years. One call. That's all it usually took. One frantic call from Hope.

No, she corrected fiercely. Not Hope. *Anne.* Although her cousin was dead, Grace had to remember to think and remember and refer to her as Anne.

She made that her mantra as the Mercedes sliced through the night. She was still repeating it when Blake pulled into the underground parking for Dalton International's headquarters building in downtown Oklahoma City. Although the clicker attached to the Mercedes's visor raised the arm, the booth attendant leaned out with cheerful greeting.

"Evenin', Mr. Dalton."

"Hi, Roy."

"Guess your brother 'n his bride are off on their honeymoon."

"Yes, they are."

"Sure wish 'em well." He leaned farther down and tipped a finger to his brow. "How're you doin', Ms. Templeton?"

She dredged up a smile. "Fine, thanks."

Grace wasn't surprised at the friendly greeting. She'd made many a trip to Dalton International's headquarters with Molly and her grandmother. Delilah had turned over control of the manufacturing empire she and Big Jake had scratched out of bare dirt to her sons. That didn't mean she'd surrendered her right to meddle as she saw fit in either DI's corporate affairs or in her sons' lives. So Delilah, with Molly and her nanny in tow, had regularly breezed into boardrooms and conferences. Just as often, she'd zoomed up to the top floor of the DI building, where her bachelor sons maintained their separate penthouse apartments.

The penthouse also boasted a luxurious guest suite for DI's visiting dignitaries. That, apparently, was where Blake had decided to plant her. Grace guessed as much when he stopped at the security desk in the lower lobby to retrieve a key card. Moments later the glass-enclosed elevator whisked them upward.

Once past the street level, Oklahoma City zoomed into view. On previous visits Grace had gasped at the skyline that rose story by eye-popping story. Tonight she barely noticed the panorama of lights and skyscrapers. Her entire focus was on the man crowding her against the elevator's glass wall.

She hadn't been able to tell which Dalton twin was which at first. With their dark gold hair, chiseled chins and broad shoulders, one was a feast for the eyes. Two of them standing side by side could make any woman drool.

It hadn't taken Grace long to separate the men. Alex was more outgoing, with a wicked grin that jump-started female hormones without him half trying. Blake was quieter. Less obvious. With a smile that was all the more seductive for being slow and warm and…

The ping of the elevator wrenched her back to the tortuous present. When the doors slid open, Blake grasped her arm again and marched her down a plushly carpeted hall toward a set of polished oak doors.

Okay, enough! Grace didn't get angry often. When she did, her temper flashed hot and fierce enough to burn through the fear still gripping her by the throat.

"That's it!" She yanked her arm free of his hold and stopped dead in the center of the hall. "You hustle me out of your mother's house like a thief caught stealing the silver. You order me into your bright, shiny convertible. You drag me up here in the middle of the night. I'm not taking another step until you stop acting like you're the Gestapo or KGB."

He arched a brow at her rant, then coolly, deliberately shot back the cuff of his pleated tux shirt to check his gold Rolex.

"It's nine-twenty-two. Hardly the middle of the night."

She wanted to hit him. Slap that stony expression right off his too-handsome face. Might have actually attempted it if she wasn't sure she would crack a couple of finger bones on his hard, unyielding jaw.

Besides which, he deserved some answers. The detective's report had obviously delivered a body blow. He'd loved her cousin once.

The fire drained from Grace's heart, leaving only sadness tinged now with an infinite weariness. "All right. I'll tell you what I can."

With a curt nod, he strode the last few feet to the guest suite. A swipe of the key card clicked the lock on the wide oak doors. Grace had visited the lavish guest suite a number of times. Each time she stepped inside, though, the sheer magnificence of the view stopped her breath in her throat.

Angled floor-to-ceiling glass walls gave a stunning, hundred-and-eighty-degree panorama of Oklahoma City's skyline. The view was spectacular during the day, offering an eagle's-eye glimpse of the domed capitol building, the Oklahoma River and the colorful barges that carried tourists past Bricktown Ballpark to the larger-than-life-size bronze sculptures commemorating the 1889 land run. That momentous event had opened some two million acres of unassigned land to settlers and, oh, by the way, created a tent city with a population of more than fifty thousand almost overnight.

The view on a clear summer night like this one was even more dazzling. Skyscrapers glowed like beacons. White lights twinkled in the trees lining the river spur that meandered through the downtown area. But it was the colossal bronze statue atop the floodlit capitol that drew Grace to the windows. She'd been born and bred in Texas, but as a social studies teacher she knew enough of the history of the Southwest to appreciate the deep symbolism in the twenty-two-foot-tall bronze statue. She'd also been given a detailed history of the statue by Delilah, who'd served on the committee that raised funds for it.

Erected in 2002, *The Guardian,* with his tall spear, muscular body and unbowed head, represented not only the thousands of Native Americans who'd been forced from their homes in the East and settled in what was then Indian Territory. The statue also embodied Oklahomans who'd wrestled pipe into red dirt as hard as brick to suck out the oil that fueled the just-born automobile industry. The sons and daughters who lived through the devastating Dust Bowl of the '30s. The proud Americans who'd worked rotating shifts at the Army Air Corps' Douglas Aircraft Plant in the '40s to overhaul, repair and build fighters and bombers. And, most recently, the grimly determined Oklahomans who'd dug through nine stories of rubble to recover the bodies of friends and coworkers killed in the Murrah Building bombing.

Grace and Hope... No! Grace and *Anne* had driven up from Texas during their junior year in high school to visit Oklahoma City's National Memorial & Museum. Neither of them had been able to comprehend how the homegrown terrorist Timothy McVeigh could be so evil, so twisted in both mind and morals. Then, less than a year later, her cousin met Jack Petrie.

Frost coated Grace's lungs. Feeling its sick chill, she wrapped both arms around her waist and turned away from *The Guardian* to face Blake Dalton.

"I can't tell you about Anne's past," she said bleakly. "I promised I would bury it with her. What I *can* say is that you're the only man she got close to in more years than you want to know."

"You think I'm going to be satisfied with that?"

"You have no choice."

"Wrong."

He yanked on the dangling end of his bow tie and threw it aside before shrugging out of his tuxedo jacket. His black satin cummerbund circled a trim waist. The pleated white shirt was still crisp, as might be expected from a tailor who catered exclusively to millionaires and movie stars.

Yet under the sleek sophistication was an edge

that didn't fool Grace for a moment. Delilah bragged constantly about the variety of sports Blake and his twin had excelled at during their school years. Both men still carried an athlete's build—lean in the hips and flanks, with the solid chest and muscled shoulders of a former collegiate wrestler.

That chest loomed far too large in Grace's view at the moment. It invaded her space, distracted her thoughts and made her distinctly nervous.

"How many cousins do you have?" he asked with silky menace. "And how long do you think it will take Jamison to check each of them out?"

"Not long," she fired back. "But he won't find anything beyond Anne's birth certificate, driver's license and a few high school yearbook photos. We made sure of that."

"A person can't just erase her entire life after high school."

"As a matter of fact, she can."

Grace moved to the buckskin leather sofa and dropped onto a cushion. Blake folded his tall frame onto a matching sofa separated by a half acre of glass-topped coffee table.

"It's not easy. Or cheap," she added, thinking of her empty savings account. "But you can pull it off with the help of a very smart friend of a friend of a friend. Especially if said friend can tap into just about any computer system."

Like the Texas Vital Statistics agency. It had taken some serious hacking but they'd managed to delete the digital entry recording Hope Patricia Templeton's marriage to Jack David Petrie. By doing so, they'd also deleted the record of the last time Grace had used her maiden name and SSN.

A familiar sadness settled like a lump in Grace's middle. Her naive, trusting cousin had believed Petrie's promise to love and cherish and provide for her every need. As the bastard had explained in the months that followed, his wife didn't require access to their bank account. Or a credit card. Or a job. Nor did she have to register to vote. There weren't any candidates worth going to that trouble for. And they sure as hell didn't need to talk to a marriage counselor, he'd added when she finally realized he'd made her a virtual prisoner.

Financially dependent and emotionally battered, she'd spent long, isolated years as a shadow person. Jack trotted her out when he wanted to display his pretty wife, then shuffled her back into her proper place in his bed. It hadn't taken him long to cut off her ties with her friends and family, either. All except Grace. She refused to be cut, even after Petrie became furious over her meddling. Grace wondered whether those horrific moments when her gas pedal locked on the interstate were, in fact, due to mechanical failure.

Grace and Hope had become more cautious after that. No more visits. No letters or emails that could be intercepted. No calls to the house. Only to a pay phone in the one grocery store where Jack allowed his wife to shop. Even then it had taken a solid year of pleading before Hope worked up the courage to escape.

Grace didn't want to remember the desperate years that followed. The mindless fear. The countless moves. The series of false identities and fake SSNs, each one more expensive to procure than the last. Until finally—*finally!*—a woman with the name of Anne Jordan had found anonymity and a tenuous, tentative security at Dalton International. She'd been just one of DI's thousands of employees worldwide. An entry-level clerk with only a high school GED. Certainly not a position that would bring her into contact with the multinational corporation's CFO.

Yet it had.

"Please, Blake. Please believe me when I tell you Anne wanted her past to be buried with her. All she cared about in her last, agonizing moments was making sure Molly would know her father, if not her mother."

Or more accurately, that her baby would have the name and protection of someone completely unknown to Jack Petrie.

Grace prayed she'd convinced Blake. She hadn't, of course. The lawyer in him wouldn't be satisfied until he'd dug up and turned over every bit of evidence. But maybe she could deflect his inquisition.

"Will you tell me something?"

"Quid pro quo?" His mouth twisted. "You haven't given me much of a trade."

"Please. I…I wasn't able to talk or visit with Anne much in her last year."

She hadn't dared. Jack Petrie was a Texas state trooper, with a cop's wide connections. Grace knew he'd had her under surveillance at various times, maybe even bugged her phone or planted a tracking device on her car, hoping she would lead him to his wife. Grace had imposed on every friend she had, borrowing their cars or using their phones, to maintain even minimal contact with her cousin.

Jack didn't know about Grace's last, frantic flight to California. She'd made sure of that. She'd emptied her savings account, had a friend drive her to the airport and paid cash for a ticket to Vegas. There she'd rented a car for a desperate drive across the desert to the San Diego hospital where her cousin had been admitted.

Five heart-wrenching days later, she'd retraced that route with Molly. Instead of flying back to San Antonio with the baby, though, she'd paid cash for a bus ticket to Oklahoma City.

She hadn't used her cell phone or any credit cards in the weeks since she'd wrangled a job as Molly's temporary nanny. Nor had she cashed the checks Delilah had written for her salary.

She'd planned to go back to her teaching job once Molly was settled with her father. The longer she spent with the baby, though, the more painful the prospect of leaving her became.

The thought of leaving Blake Dalton was almost as wrenching. Lately her mind had drifted to him more than it should. Especially at night, after she'd put Molly to bed. The increasingly erotic direction of that drift spurred pinpricks of guilt, then and now.

"Tell me how you and Anne met," she pleaded, reminding herself yet again Blake was her cousin's love, the man she'd let into her life despite all she'd been through. "How... Well..."

"How Molly happened?" he supplied.

"Yes. Anne was so shy around men."

For shy, read insecure and cowed and generally scared *shitless*. Grace couldn't imagine how Blake had breached those formidable barriers.

"Please," she said softly. "Tell me. I'd like to know she found a little happiness before she died."

He stared at her for long moments, then his breath eased out on a sigh.

"I think she was happy for the few weeks we were together. I was never sure, though. Took me forever to pry more than a murmured hello from her. Even after I got her to agree to go out with me, she didn't want anyone at DI to know we were seeing each other. Said it would look bad, the big boss dating a lowly file clerk."

He hooked his wrists on his knees and contemplated his black dress shoes. He must not have liked what he saw. A note of unmistakable self-disgust colored his deep voice.

"She wouldn't let me take her to dinner or to the theater or anywhere we might be seen together. It was always her place. Or a hotel."

It had to be that, Grace knew. Her cousin couldn't take the chance some society reporter or gossip columnist would start fanning rumors about rich, handsome Blake Dalton's latest love interest. Or worse, the paparazzi might snap a photo of them together and post it on the internet.

Yet she risked going to a hotel with him. She'd come out of her defensive crouch enough for that. And when she discovered she was pregnant with his child, she'd had no choice but to run away.

She wanted the baby desperately, but she couldn't tell Dalton about the pregnancy. He would have wanted to give the child his name, or at least establish his legal rights as the father. Hope's false IDs wouldn't have held up under legal scrutiny, and her real one would have led Petrie to her. So she'd run. Again.

"Did you love her?"

Damn! Grace hadn't meant to let that slip out. And she sure as heck hadn't intended to feel jealous of her cousin's relationship with this man.

Yet she knew he had to have been so tender with her. So sensitive to her needs. His mouth would have played a gentle song on her skin. His hands, those strong, tanned hands, must have stroked and soothed even as they aroused and…

"I don't know."

With a flush of guilt, Grace jerked her attention back to his face.

"I cared for her," he said quietly, as much to himself as to her. "Enough to press her into going to bed with me. But when she left without a word, I was angry as well as hurt."

Regret and remorse chased each other across his face.

"Then, when I got the report of the bus accident…"

He stopped and directed a look of fierce accusation at Grace.

"I wasn't with her when it happened," she said in feeble self-defense. "She was by herself, in her car. The bus spun out right in front of her and hit a bridge abutment. She was terrified, but she got out to help."

"And left her purse at the scene."

"Yes."

"Deliberately?"

"Yes."

"Why?"

Grace shook her head. "I can't tell you why. I can't tell you any more than I have. I promised Anne her past would die with her."

"But it didn't," he countered swiftly. "Molly's living proof of that."

She slipped off the sofa and onto her knees, desperate for him to let it go. "She's your daughter, Blake. Please, just accept that and take joy in her."

He was silent for so long she didn't think he would respond. When he did, the ice was back in his voice.

"All I have right now is your word that Anne and I had a child together. I'll send in the DNA sample you offered to provide. Once we have the results, we'll discuss where we go from here."

"Where I need to go is back to your mother's house! She's exhausted from the wedding. She told me tonight she was feeling every one of her sixty-two years. She can't take care of Molly by herself for the next few days."

"I'll help her, and when I can't be there I'll make sure someone else is. In the meantime, you stay put."

He pushed out of the chair and strode to the wet bar built into the far wall. For a moment Grace thought he intended to pour them both a drink to wash down the hurt and bitterness of the past hour, but he lifted only one crystal tumbler from one of the mirrored shelves. He returned with it and issued a terse command.

"Spit."

Three

The melodic chimes of a doorbell pierced Grace's groggy haze. When the chimes gave way to the hammer of an impatient fist, she propped herself up on one elbow and blinked at the digital clock beside the bed.

Oh, God! Seven-twenty! She'd slept right through Molly's first feeding.

She threw the covers aside and was half out of bed before reality hit. One, this wasn't her room in Delilah's mansion. Two, she was wearing only the lavender lace bikini briefs she left on when she'd changed her maid of honor gown.

And three, she was no longer Molly's temporary nanny.

Last night's agonizing events came crashing down on her as the fist hammered again. Scrambling, Grace snatched up her now hopelessly wrinkled khaki crops and white blouse. She got the pants zipped and buttoned the blouse on her way to the front door. She had a good idea whose fist was pounding away. She'd spent almost a month now with Blake Dalton's often autocratic, occasionally irascible, always kind-hearted mother.

So she expected to see the raven-haired matriarch. She *didn't* expect to see the baby riding on Delilah's chest, nested contentedly in a giraffe sling. Grace gripped the brass door latch, swamped by an avalanche of love and worry and guilt as she dragged her gaze from the infant to her grandmother.

"Delilah, I…"

"Don't you Delilah me!" She stomped inside, the soles of her high-topped sneakers slapping the marble foyer. "Don't you dare Delilah me!"

Grace closed the door and followed her into the

living room. She wished she'd taken a few seconds to brush her hair and slap some water on her face before this showdown. And coffee! She needed coffee. Desperately.

She'd tossed and turned most of the night. The few hours she'd drifted into a doze, she'd dreamed of Anne. And Blake. Grace had been there, too, stunned when his fury at her swirled without warning into a passion that jerked her awake, breathless and wanting. Remnants of that mindless hunger still drifted like a steamy haze through her mind as Delilah slung a diaper bag from her shoulder onto the sofa and released Molly from the sling.

Grace couldn't help but note that her employer had gone all jungle today. The diaper bag was zebra-striped. Grinning monkeys frolicked and swung from vines on the baby's seersucker dress. Delilah herself was in knee-length leopard tights topped by an oversize black T-shirt with a neon message urging folks to come out and be amazed by Oklahoma City's new gorilla habitat—a habitat she'd coaxed, cajoled and strong-armed her friends into funding.

"Don't just stand there," she snapped at Grace. "Get the blanket out of the diaper bag."

Even the blanket was a riot of green and yellow and jungle red. Grace spread it a safe distance away from the glass coffee table. Molly was just learning to crawl. She could push herself onto her hands and knees and hold her head up to survey the world with bright, inquisitive eyes.

Delilah deposited the baby on the blanket and made sure she was centered before pointing an imperious finger at Grace.

"You. Sit." The older woman plunked herself down in the opposite chair, keeping the baby between them. "Now talk."

"You sure you wouldn't like some coffee first?" Grace asked with a hopeful glance at the suite's fully equipped kitchen. "I could make a quick pot."

"Screw coffee. Talk."

Grace blew out a sigh and raked her fingers through her unbrushed hair. Obviously Delilah had no intention of making this easy.

"I don't know how much Blake told you..." She let that dangle for a moment. Got no response.

"Okay, here's the condensed version. Molly's mother was my cousin. When Anne worked at Dalton International, she had a brief affair with your son. She died before she could tell me *which* son, so I brought Molly to you and finessed a job as her nanny while Alex and Blake sorted out the paternity issue."

Delilah pinned Grace with a look that could have etched steel. "If one of my sons got this cousin of yours pregnant, why didn't she have the guts or the decency to let him know about the baby?"

Grace stiffened. Shielding Hope—*Anne!*— had become as much a part of her as breathing. No one knew what her cousin had endured. And Grace was damned if she'd allow anyone, even the formidable Delilah Dalton, to put her down.

"I told Blake and I'll tell you. Anne had good reasons for what she did, but she wanted those reasons to die with her. She didn't, however, want her baby to grow up without knowing either of her parents."

Delilah fired back with both barrels. "Don't get uppity with me, girl!"

The fierce retort startled the baby. Molly swung her head toward her grandmother, wobbled and plopped down on one diapered hip. Both women instinctively bent toward her, but she was already pushing back onto her knees.

Delilah moderated her tone if not her message. "I'm the one who bought your out-of-work schoolteacher story, remember? I took you into my home. I trusted you, dammit."

Grace didn't see any use in pointing out that she hadn't lied about being a teacher or temporarily out of work. The trust part stung enough.

"I'm sorry I couldn't tell you about my connection to Molly."

"Ha!"

"I promised my cousin I would make sure her child was loved and cared for." Her glance went again to the baby, happily drooling and rocking on hands and knees. Slowly, she brought her gaze back to Delilah. "And she is," Grace said softly. "Well cared for and very much loved."

Delilah huffed out something close to a snort but didn't comment for long moments. "I pride myself on being a good judge of character," she said at last. "Even that horny goat I married lived up to almost everything I'd expected of him."

Grace didn't touch that one. She'd heard Delilah say more than once she wished to hell Big Jake Dalton hadn't died before she'd found out about his little gal pal. His passing would've been a lot less peaceful.

"Is all this you've just told me true?" the Dalton matriarch demanded.

"Yes, ma'am."

"Molly's mother was really your cousin?"

"Yes."

"Well, I guess we'll have proof of that soon enough. Damned lab is making a fortune off all these rush DNA tests we've ordered lately."

She pooched her lips and moved them from side to side before coming to an abrupt decision.

"I've watched you with Molly. I don't believe you're some schemer looking to extort big bucks from us. You'll have to work to convince Blake of that, though."

"I can't tell him any more than I have."

"You don't know him like I do. He has his ways of getting what he wants. So do I," she added as she pushed out of the chair and adjusted the sling. "So do I. C'mon, Mol, let's go see your daddy."

Without thinking Grace moved to help. Swooping the baby up, she planted wet, sloppy kisses on her cheeks before slipping the infant's feet through the sling's leg openings. While Delilah tightened the straps, Grace folded the jungle blanket back into the diaper bag and handed it to the older woman.

"I'm sorry Blake doesn't want me to help with Molly."

"We'll manage until this mess gets sorted out."

If it got sorted out. Grace grew more antsy as one day stretched into two, then three.

Blake had her things packed and delivered along with her purse. She tried to take that as a good sign. Apparently he wasn't afraid she would pull a disappearing act like her cousin had.

He didn't contact her personally, though, and that worried Grace. It also caused an annoyingly persistent ache. Only now that she'd been banished from their lives did she realize how attached she'd become to the Daltons, mother and son. And to Molly! Grace missed cooing to the baby and watching her count her toes and shampooing her soft, downy blond hair.

She'd known the time would come when she would have to drop out of Molly's life. The longer she stayed here, the greater the risk Jack Petrie might trace her to Oklahoma City and wonder what she was doing here. Yet she felt a sharp pang of dismay when Blake finally condescended to call a little past 6:00 p.m. with a curt announcement.

"I need to talk to you."

"All right."

"I'm downstairs," he informed her. "I'll be up in a few minutes."

At least she was a little better prepared for this face-to-face than she'd been for their last. Her hair was caught up in a smooth knot and she'd swiped on some lip gloss earlier. She debated whether to change her jeans and faded San Antonio SeaWorld T-shirt but decided to use the time to take deep, calming breaths.

Not that they did much good. The Blake Dalton she opened the door to wasn't one she'd seen before. He'd always appeared at his mother's house in suits or neatly pressed shirts and slacks sporting creases sharp enough to shave fuzz from a peach. Then, of course, there was the tux he'd donned for the wedding. Armani should wish for male models with builds like either of the Dalton twins.

This Blake was considerably less refined. Faded jeans rode low on his hips. A black T-shirt stretched across his taut shoulders. Bristles the same shade of amber as his hair shadowed his cheeks and chin. He looked tough and uncompromising, but the expression in his laser blues wasn't as cold as the one he'd worn at their last meeting, thank God.

"We got the lab report back."

Wordlessly she led the way into the living room. Electric screens shielded the wall of windows from the sun that hadn't yet slipped down behind the skyscrapers. Without the endless view, the room seemed smaller, more intimate. *Too* intimate, she decided when she turned and found Blake had stopped mere inches away.

"Aren't you going to ask the results?"

"I don't need to," she said with a shrug. "Unless the lab screwed up the samples, their report confirms Molly and I descend from the same family tree."

"They didn't screw up the samples."

"Okay." She crossed her arms. "Now what?"

Surprise flickered across his face.

"What'd you expect?" Grace asked, her chin angling. "That I would throw myself into your arms for finally acknowledging the truth?"

The surprise was still there, but then his gaze dropped to her mouth and it took on a different quality. Darker. More intense. As though the idea of Grace throwing herself at him was less of a shock than something to be considered, evaluated, assessed.

Now that the idea was out there, it didn't particularly shock her, either. Just the opposite. In fact, the urge grew stronger with each second it floated around in the realm of possibility. All she had to do was step forward. Slide her palms over his shoulders. Lean into his strength.

As her cousin had.

Guilt sent Grace back a pace, not forward. He'd

been Anne's lover, she reminded herself fiercely. The father of her baby. At best, Grace was a problem he was being forced to solve.

"Now you know," she said with a shrug that disguised her true feelings. "You're Molly's father. And *I* know you'll be good with her. So it's time for me to pack and head back to San Antonio. I'll stop by to say goodbye to her on my way out of town."

"That's it?" His frown deepened. "You're just going to drop out of her life?"

"I'll see her when I can."

After she was certain Jack Petrie hadn't learned about her stay in Oklahoma City.

"There are legalities that have to be attended to," Blake protested. "I'll need Molly's birth certificate. Her mother's death certificate."

Both contained the false name and SSN her cousin had used in California. Grace could only pray the documents would be sufficient for Blake's needs. They should. With his legal connections and his family's political clout here in Oklahoma, he ought to be able to push whatever he wanted through the courts.

"I'll send you copies," she promised.

"Right." He paused, his jaw working. "I hope you know that whatever trouble Anne was in, I would have helped her."

"Yes," she said softly. "I know."

His eyes searched hers. "Anne couldn't bring herself to trust me, but you can, Grace."

She wanted to. God, how she wanted to! Somehow she managed to swallow the hard lump in her throat.

"I trust you to cherish Molly."

Saying goodbye to the baby was every bit as hard as it had been to say goodbye to Blake. Molly broke into delighted coos when she saw her nanny and lifted both arms, demanding to be cuddled.

Grace refused to cry until her rental car was on I-35 and heading south. Tears blurred the rolling Oklahoma countryside for the next fifty miles. By the time she crossed the Red River into Texas, her throat was raw and her eyes so puffy that she had to stop at the welcome center to douse them with cold water. Six hours later she hit the outskirts of San Antonio, still mourning her severed ties to Molly and the woman who'd been both cousin and best friend to her since earliest childhood.

Her tiny condo in one of the city's older suburbs felt stale and stuffy when she let herself in. With a gulp, she glanced from the living room she'd painted a warm terra-cotta to the closet-size kitchen. She loved her place, but the entire two-bedroom unit could fit in the foyer of Delilah Dalton's palatial mansion.

As soon as she'd unpacked and powered up her computer, Grace scanned the certificates she'd promised to send Blake. That done, she skimmed through the hundreds of emails that had piled up in her absence and tried to pick up the pieces of her life.

The next two weeks dragged interminably. School didn't start until the end of month. Unfortunately, the open-ended leave of absence Grace had requested had forced her principal to shuffle teachers to cover the fall semester. The best he could promise was hopefully steady work as a substitute until after Christmas.

At loose ends until school started, Grace had to cut as many corners as possible to make up for her depleted bank account. Even worse, she missed Molly more than she would have believed possible. The baby had taken up permanent residence in her heart.

Only at odd moments would she admit she missed Molly's father almost as much as she did the baby. Like everyone else swept up in the Daltons' orbit, she'd been overwhelmed by Delilah's forceful personality and dazzled by Alex's wicked grin and audacious charm. Now that she viewed the Dalton clan from a distance, however, Grace recognized Blake as the brick and mortar keeping the family together. Always there when his mother needed him to pull together the financing on yet another of her charitable ventures. Holding the reins at Dalton International's corporate headquarters while Alex jetted halfway around the world to consult with suppliers or customers. Grace missed seeing his tall form across the table at his mother's house, missed hearing his delighted chuckle when he tickled Molly's tummy and got her giggling.

The only bright spot in those last, endless days of summer was that she heard nothing from Jack Petrie. She began to breathe easy again, convinced she'd covered her tracks. That false sense of security lasted right up until she answered the doorbell on a rainy afternoon.

When she peered though the peephole, the shock of seeing who stood on the other side dropped her jaw. A second later, fear exploded in her chest. Her fingers scrabbled for the dead bolt. She got it unlocked and threw the door almost back on its hinges.

"Blake!"

He had to step back to keep from getting slammed by the glass storm door. Grace barely registered the neat black slacks, the white button-down shirt with the open collar and sleeves rolled up, the hair burnished to dark, gleaming gold by rain.

"Is...?" Her heart hammered. Her voice shook. "Is Molly okay?"

"No."

"Oh, God!" A dozen horrific scenarios spun through her head. "What happened?"

"She misses you."

Grace gaped at him stupidly. "What?"

"She misses you. She's been fretting since you left. Mother says she's teething."

The disaster scenes faded. Molly wasn't injured. She hadn't been kidnapped. Almost reeling with relief, Grace sagged against the doorjamb.

"That's what you came down to San Antonio to tell me?" she asked incredulously. "Molly's teething?"

"That, and the fact that she said her first word."

And Grace had missed both events! The loss hit like a blow as Blake's glance went past her and swept the comfortable living room.

"May I come in?"

"Huh? Oh. Yes, of course."

She moved inside, all too conscious now of her bare feet and the T-shirt hacked off to her midriff. The shirt topped a pair of ragged cutoffs that skimmed her butt cheeks.

The cutoffs were comfortable in the cozy privacy of her home but nothing she would have ever considered wearing while she'd worked for Delilah—or around her son. She caught Blake's gaze tracking to her legs, moving upward. Disconcerted by the sudden heat that slow once-over generated, she gulped and snatched at his reason for being there.

"What did Molly say?"

"We thought it was just a ga-ga," he said with a small, almost reluctant smile. "Mother insisted she was trying to say ga-ma, but it came out on a hiss."

She sounded it out in her head, and felt her stomach go hard and tight.

"Gace? Molly said Gace?"

"Several times now."

"I…uh…"

He waited a beat, but she couldn't pull it together enough for coherence. She was too lost in the stinging regret of missing those first words.

"We want you to come back, Grace."

Startled, she looked up to find Blake regarding her intently.

"Who's *we?*" she stammered.

"All of us. Mother, me, Julie and Alex."

"They're back from their honeymoon?"

"They flew in last night."

"And you…" She had to stop and suck in a shaky breath. "And you want me to come back and pick up where I left off as Molly's nanny?"

"Not as her nanny. As my wife."

Four

Blake could certainly understand Grace's slack-jawed astonishment. He'd spent the entire flight to San Antonio telling himself it was insane to propose marriage to a woman who refused to trust him with the truth.

It was even more insane for him to miss her the way he had. She'd wormed her way into his mother's house and Molly's heart. She'd lied to him—to all of them—by omission if nothing else. Yet the hole she'd left behind had grown deeper with each hour she was gone.

Molly's unexpected arrival had already turned his calm, comfortable routine upside down. This doe-eyed blonde had kicked it all to hell. So he felt a savage satisfaction to see his own chaotic feelings mirrored in her face.

"You're crazy! I can't marry you!"

"Why not?"

She was sputtering, almost incoherent. "Because... Because..."

He thought she might break down and tell him then. Trust him with the truth. When she didn't, he swallowed a bitter pill of disappointment.

"Why don't we sit down?" he suggested with a calm he was far from feeling. "Talk this through."

"Talk it through?" She gave a bubble of hysterical laughter and swept a hand toward the living room. "My first marriage proposal, and he wants to *talk* it though. By all means, counselor, have a seat."

She regrouped during the few moments it took him to move to a sofa upholstered in a nubby plaid that complemented the earth-toned walls and framed prints of Roman antiquities. As she dropped into a chair facing him, Blake could see her astonishment giving way to anger. The first hints of it fired her eyes and stiffened her shoulders under her cottony T-shirt. He had to work to keep his gaze from drifting to the expanse of creamy skin exposed by the shirt's hem. And those legs. Christ!

He'd better remember what he'd come for. He had to approach this challenge the same way he did all others. Coolly and logically.

"I've had time to think since you left, Grace. You're good with Molly. So good both she and my mother have had difficulty adjusting to your absence."

So had he, dammit. It irritated Blake to no end that he hadn't been able to shut this woman out of his head. She'd lied to him and stubbornly refused to trust him. Yet he'd found himself making excuses for the lies and growing more determined by the hour to convince her to open up.

"You're also Molly's closest blood relative on her mother's side," he continued.

As far as he could determine at this point, anyway. He fully intended to keep digging. Whatever it took, however he got it, he wanted the truth.

"That's right," she confirmed with obvious reluctance. "Anne's parents are dead, and she was their only child."

He waited, willing her to share another scrap of information about her cousin. It hit Blake then that he could barely remember what Anne had looked like. They'd been together such a short time—if those few, furtive meetings outside their work environment could be termed togetherness.

Jaw locked, he tried to summon her image. She'd been an inch or two shorter than Grace. That much he remembered. And her eyes were several shades darker than her cousin's warm, caramel-brown. Beyond that, she was a faint memory when compared with the vibrant female now facing him.

Torn between guilt and regret, Blake presented his next argument. "I know you're facing monetary problems right now."

She bolted upright in her chair. "What'd you do? Have Jamison check my financials?"

"Yes." He offered no apology. "I'm guessing you drained your resources to help Anne and Molly. I owe you for that, Grace."

"Enough to marry me?" she bit out.

"That's part of the equation." He hesitated, aware he was about to enter treacherous territory. "There's another consideration, of course. Something frightened Anne enough to send her into hiding. It has to frighten you, too, or you wouldn't have gone to such lengths to protect her."

He'd struck a nerve. He could tell by the way she wouldn't meet his eyes. Regret that he hadn't been able to shield Anne from whoever or whatever had threatened her knifed into him. With it came an implacable determination to protect Grace. Battling the fierce urge to shake the truth out of her, he offered her not just his name but every powerful resource at his disposal.

"I'll take care of you," he promised, his steady gaze holding hers. "You *and* Molly."

She wanted to yield. He could see it in her eyes. He congratulated himself, reveling in the potent mix of satisfaction at winning her confidence and a primal need to protect his chosen mate.

His fierce exultation didn't last long. Only until she shook her head.

"I appreciate the offer, Blake. You don't know how much. But I can take care of myself."

He hadn't realized until that moment how determined he was to put his ring on her finger. His expression hardening, he played his trump card.

"There's another aspect to consider. Right now, you can't—or won't—claim any degree of kinship to Molly. That could impact your access to her."

Her back went rigid. "What are you saying? That you wouldn't let me see her if I don't marry you?"

"No. I'm simply pointing out that you have no legal rights where she's concerned. Mother's not getting any younger," he reminded her coolly. "And if something should happen to me or Alex..."

He was too good an attorney to overstate his case. Shrugging, he let her mull over the possibilities.

Grace did, with ever increasing indignation. She couldn't believe it! He'd trapped her in her own web of lies and half-truths. If she wanted to see Molly—which she did, desperately!—she would have to play the game by his rules.

But marriage? Could she tie her future to his for the sake of the baby? The prospect dismayed her enough to produce a sharp round of questions.

"What about love, Blake? And sex? And everything else that goes into a marriage? Don't you want that?"

With a smooth move, he pushed off the sofa. Grace rose hastily as well and was almost prepared when he stopped mere inches away.

"Do you?" he asked.

"Of course I do!"

For the first time she saw a glint of humor in his eyes. "Then I don't see a problem. The sex is certainly doable. We can work on the love."

Dammit! She couldn't form a coherent thought with him standing so close. Between that and the blood pounding in her ears, she was forced to fight for every breath. It had to be oxygen deprivation that made her agree to his outrageous proposal.

"All right, counselor. You've made your case. I want to be part of Molly's life. I'll marry you."

She thought that would elicit a positive response. At least a nod. Wasn't that what he wanted? What he'd flown down here for? So why the hell did his brows snap together and he looked as though he seriously regretted his offer?

Let them snap! They'd both gone too far to back down now. But there was one final gauntlet she had to throw down.

"I just have one condition."

"And that is?"

"We play this marriage very low-key. No formal announcement. No fancy ceremony. No big, expensive reception with pictures splashed across the society page."

She paced the room, thinking furiously. She'd covered her tracks in Oklahoma City. She was sure of it. Still, it was best to stick as close to the truth as possible.

"If anyone asks, we met several months ago. Fell in love, but needed time to be sure. Decided it was for real when you flew down here to see me this weekend, so we found a justice of the peace and did the deed. Period. End of story."

She turned, hands on hips, and waited for his response. It was slow coming. *Extremely* slow.

"Well?" she demanded, refusing to let his stony silence unnerve her. "Do we have a deal or don't we?"

He held out a hand. To shake on their bargain, she realized as the full ramifications of what she'd just agreed to sank in. If her cousin's horrific experience hadn't killed most of Grace's girlish fantasies about marriage, this coolly negotiated business arrangement would have done the trick.

Except Blake didn't take the hand she extended. To her surprise, he elbowed her arm aside, hooked her waist and brought her up against his chest.

"If we're going to project a pretense of being in love, we'd better practice for the cameras."

"No! No cameras, remember? No splashy... Mmmmph!"

She ended on a strangled note as his mouth came down on hers. The kiss was harder than it needed to be. It was also everything that she'd imagined it might be! Her blood leaping, she gloried in the press of his body against hers for a moment or two or ten.

Then reality hit. This was payback for the secrets she still refused to reveal. A taste of the sex he'd so generously offered to provide. She bristled, fully intending to jerk out of his hold, but he moved first.

Dropping his arm, he put a few inches between them. He'd lost that granite look, but she wasn't sure she liked the self-disgust much better.

"I'm sorry."

"You should be," she threw back. "Manhandling me isn't part of our deal."

"You're right. That was uncalled for."

It certainly was. Yet for some perverse reason, the apology irritated her more than the kiss.

"Do we need to negotiate an addendum?" she asked acidly. "Something to the effect that physical contact must be mutually agreed to?"

Red singed his cheeks. "Amendment accepted. If you still want to go through with the contract, that is."

"Do you?"

"Yes."

"Then I do, too."

"Fine." His glance swept over her, lingering again momentarily on her legs. "You'd better get changed."

"Excuse me?"

"You scripted the scenario. I flew down to see you. We decided it was for real. We hunted down a justice of the peace. Period. End of story."

She threw an incredulous glance at the window. Rain still banged against the panes. Thunder rumbled in the distance.

"You want to get married *today?*"

"Why not?"

She could think of a hundred reasons, not least of which was the fact that she had yet to completely recover from that kiss.

"What about blood tests?" she protested. "The seventy-two-hour mandatory waiting period?"

"Texas doesn't require blood tests. I've checked."

Of course he had.

"And the seventy-two-hour waiting period can be waived if you know the right people."

Which he did. Grace should have known he

would cover every contingency with his usual attention to detail.

"We'll get the marriage license at the Bexar County Courthouse. One of my father's old cronies is a circuit judge. I'll call and see if he's available to perform the ceremony." He pulled out his cell phone. "Pack what you need to take back to Oklahoma with you. We'll arrange for a moving company to take care of the rest."

The speed of it, the meticulous preplanning and swift execution, left her breathless.

"You were that sure of me?" she asked, feeling dazed and off balance.

He paused in the act of scrolling through the phone's address book. "I was that sure of how much you love Molly."

They left for the county courthouse a little more than three hours later. Blake was driving the Lincoln town car his efficient staff had arranged for him. As Grace stared through the Lincoln's rain-streaked window, she grappled with a growing sense of unreality.

Like all young girls, she and her cousin had

spent hours with an old lace tablecloth wrapped around their shoulders, playing bride. During giggly sleepovers, they'd imagined numerous iterations of her wedding day. Grace's favorite consisted of a church fragrant with flowers and perfumed candles, a radiant bride in filmy white and friends packed into the pews.

After that came the smaller, more intimate version. Just her, her cousin as her attendant, a handsome groom and the pastor in a shingle-roofed gazebo while her family beamed from white plastic folding chairs. She'd even toyed occasionally with the idea of Elvis walking her down the aisle in one of Vegas's wedding chapels. This hurried, unromantic version had never figured in her imagination, however.

The reality of it hit home when they walked across a rain-washed plaza to the Bexar County Courthouse. The building was listed on the National Register of Historic Places. Unfortunately the recent storm and still ominous thunderclouds hanging low in an angry sky tinted its sandstone turrets to prison-gray. The edifice looked both drab and foreboding as Blake escorted Grace up its granite steps.

The frosted window on the door of the county clerk's office welcomed walk-ins, but the bored counter attendant showed little interest in their application. He cracked a jaw-popping yawn when the prospective bride and groom filled out the application. Five minutes and thirty-five dollars later, they entered the chambers of Judge Victor Honeywell. *His* clerk, at least, seemed to feel some sense of the occasion.

The beaming, well-endowed matron hurried around her desk to shake their hands. "I can't remember the last time we got to perform a spur-of-the-moment wedding. Brides today seem to take a year just to decide on their gown."

Unlike Grace, who had slithered out of her cutoffs and into the white linen sundress she'd picked up on sale a few weeks ago.

Blake, on the other hand, had come prepared for every eventuality, a wedding included. While she'd packed, he'd retrieved a suit bag from the Lincoln. Dark worsted wool now molded his wide shoulders. An Italian silk tie that probably cost more than Grace had earned in a week was tied in a neat Windsor. The clerk's admiring gaze lingered on both shoulders and tie for noticeable moments before she turned to the bride.

"These just came for you."

She ducked behind a side counter and popped up again with a cellophane-wrapped cascade of white roses. Silver lace and sprays of white baby's breath framed the bouquet. A two-inch-wide strip of blue was looped into a floppy bow around the stems.

"The ribbon—such as it is—is the belt from my raincoat," she said, her eyes twinkling. "You know, something borrowed, something blue."

A lump blocked Grace's throat. She had to push air past it as she folded back the cellophane and traced a finger over the petals. "Thank you."

"You're welcome. And this is for you." Still beaming, the clerk pinned a white rose to Blake's lapel. "There! Now I'll take you to Judge Honeywell."

She ushered them into a set of chambers groaning with oak panels and red damask drapes. The flags of the United States and the state of Texas flanked a desk the size of a soccer field. A set of steer horns stretched across an eight-foot swath of wall behind the desk.

"It's Ms. Templeton and Mr. Dalton, Your Honor."

The man ensconced on what Grace could only term a leather throne jumped up. His black robe flapped as he rounded his desk, displaying a pair of hand-tooled cowboy boots. He was at least six-three or four and as whiskery as he was tall. When he thrust out a thorny palm, Blake had to tilt back to keep from getting stabbed by the exaggerated point of his stiff-as-a-spear handlebar mustache.

"Well, damn! So you're Big Jake Dalton's boy."

"One of them," Blake replied with a smile.

"He ever tell you 'bout the time the two of us busted up a saloon down to Nogales?"

"No, he didn't."

"Good. Some tales are best left untold." Honeywell shifted his squinty gaze to Grace. "I'd warn you against marrying up with any son of Big Jake if they didn't have the prettiest, smartest female in all fifty states for their mama." His nose twitched above the bushy mustache. "Speaking of Delilah, is she comin' to witness the ceremony?"

"No, but my brother is."

That was the first Grace had heard of it! She glanced at him in surprise while he confirmed the startling news.

"Alex should be here any moment. He was on final approach when we left the condo. In fact…"

He cocked his head. Grace followed suit and picked up the sound of footsteps in the tiled hallway. A moment later the judge's clerk reappeared with another couple in tow. The tall, tawny-haired male who entered the chambers was a mirror image of Blake. The copper-haired female with him elicited a joyous cry from Grace.

"Julie!"

She took an instinctive step toward the woman she'd grown so close to during her sojourn in Oklahoma. Guilt brought her to a dead stop. Grace hadn't lied to Julie or the Daltons, but she hadn't told the truth, either. Alex and his new wife had to be feeling the same anger Blake had when he'd first discovered her deception.

It wasn't anger she saw in her friend's distinctive green-brown eyes, however, but regret and exasperation.

"Grace, you idiot!" Brushing past Blake, Julie folded Grace into a fierce hug, roses and all. "You didn't need to go through what you did alone. You could have told me. I would've kept your secret."

Limp with relief, Grace gulped back a near sob. "The secret isn't mine to tell."

Her gaze slid to Blake's brother. Alex didn't appear quite as forgiving as his bride. She didn't blame him. She'd watched him interact with Molly these past months, knew he loved the baby every bit as much as Blake did. It had to hurt to transition so abruptly from possible father to uncle. Grace could offer only a soft apology.

"I'm sorry, Alex. I didn't know which of you was Molly's father. Honestly. Not until I'd been in Oklahoma City for a while, and by then you and Julie were, ah, working a separate set of issues."

The hard set to his jaw relaxed a fraction. "That's one way to describe the hell this stubborn woman put me through."

He stood for a moment, studying Grace's face.

She braced herself, but his next words didn't carry either the condemnation or the sting she expected.

"Everyone, me included, will tell you that my brother is the better man. But once he sets his mind to something, he can be as ruthless as I am and as hardheaded as our mother. Blake's convinced us this marriage is what he wants. Is it what you want?"

Her fingers tightened on the stem of the roses. Their white velvet scent drifted upward as she turned to her groom. Blake stood tall and seemingly at ease, but his blue eyes were locked on hers.

"Yes," she said after only a minuscule hesitation. "I'm sure."

Was that satisfaction or relief or a brief flash of panic that rippled across his face? Grace was still trying to decide when the judge boomed out instructions.

"All right, folks. Y'all gather round so we can get these two hitched."

Blake held out a hand. Grace laid her palm in his, hoping he couldn't hear the violent thump of her heart against her ribs. As they faced the judge, she reminded herself she was doing this for Molly.

Mostly.

Five

It was actually happening. It was for real. Grace had to fight the urge to pinch herself as Blake slid a band of channel-cut diamonds onto her ring finger. Dazed, she heard the judge's prompt.

"With this ring…"

Her groom followed the cues in a deep, sure voice. "With this ring…"

"I thee wed."

"I thee wed."

The diamonds caught the light from the overhead lighting. Brilliant, multicolored sparks danced and dazzled. Grace couldn't begin to guess how many carats banded her finger. Four?

Five? And she couldn't reciprocate with so much as a plain gold band.

"By the authority vested in me by the state of Texas," Judge Honeywell intoned, "I now pronounce you husband and wife."

He waited a beat before issuing another prompt. "Go ahead, Dalton. Kiss your bride."

For the second time that afternoon, Blake slipped an arm around her waist. Grace's pulse skittered. A shiver raced down her spine. Apprehension? Anticipation?

She knew which even before he bent toward her. Her whole body quivered in expectation. He was gentle this time, though. *Too* gentle! She ached to lean into him, but the deal they'd struck kept her rigid. Their marriage was first and foremost a business arrangement, a legal partnership with Molly as the focus. Grace might eventually accept Blake's oh-so-casual offer of sex, but she'd damned well better keep a close watch on her heart.

With that resolve firm in her mind, she accepted the hearty congratulations of Judge Honeywell, another fierce hug from Julie and a kiss on the cheek from her new brother-in-law. At that point Alex produced an envelope from his inside suit coat pocket.

"Mother wanted to be here, but Molly's cutting a tooth and was too fussy to fly. She sent this instead."

Grace took the envelope with some trepidation. Inside was a folded sheet of notepaper embossed with Delilah's raised monogram. Before unfolding the note, she looked a question at Blake. His small shrug told her this was as much a surprise to him as it was to her. Nervously, Grace skimmed the almost indecipherable scrawl.

I can't say I'm happy with the way you decided to do this. We'll discuss it when you get back from France. DI's corporate jet will fly you to Marseille. Contact Madame LeBlanc when you arrive. Blake has her number. Julie, Alex and I will take care of Molly.

For a wild moment Grace thought she was being hustled out of the country so Delilah could hammer some sense into Blake. Then the last line sank in. Julie, Alex and Delilah would care for Molly. She and her groom, apparently, were jetting off to France.

Wordlessly, she handed the note to Blake. After a quick read, he speared a glance at this twin. "Were you in on this?"

"I figured something was up when Mother had me ferry the Gulfstream V down to San Antonio. Where's she proposing it take you?"

"The south of France."

That produced a quick grin. "You get no sympathy from me, Bubba. She sent Julie and me to Tuscany on our wedding night. Good thing we're both pilots and know how to beat jet lag." He winked at his wife before addressing Grace. "Hope you have a passport."

"I do, but..."

But what? She'd decided in a scant few moments to turn her whole world upside down by accepting Blake's proposition. What possible objection could she have to capping an unreal marriage with a fake honeymoon?

"But Blake probably didn't bring his," she finished helplessly.

"He didn't," Julie interjected, fishing in her purse. "I did, however. Delilah had me race over and pick it up from your executive assistant," she explained as she slapped the passport into her brother-in-law's palm. "I forgot I had it until this moment."

He fingered the gold lettering for several moments, then shrugged. "Good thing you're packed," he said to Grace. "I can pick up whatever extras I need when we get to France."

They said their goodbyes at the airport. Then Alex and Julie boarded the smaller Dalton International jet that had flown Blake to San Antonio and the newlyweds crossed the tarmac to the larger, twin-engine Gulfstream V.

The captain met them at planeside and tendered his sincere best wishes. "Congratulations, Mrs. Dalton."

"I...uh... Thank you."

Blake stepped in to cover his wife's surprise at hearing herself addressed by her new title. "I understand you just got back from Tuscany, Joe. Sorry you had to make such a quick turnaround."

"Not a problem. Alex and Julie were at the controls for most of the flight back, so the crew is rested and ready to go. We'll top off our gas in New York and have you basking in the sun a mere seven hours after that."

Blake made the swift mental calculation. Three hours to New York. Seven hours to cross the Atlantic. Another hour or more to contact Madame LeBlanc and travel to the villa DI maintained in Provence. Eight hours' time difference.

He was used to transatlantic flights, but he suspected Grace would be dead by the time they arrived at their final destination. Just as well. She could use the next few days to rest and get used to the idea of marriage.

So could he, for that matter. He'd lined up all his arguments, pro and con, before he'd flown down to San Antonio. Then Grace had opened the door in those cutoffs and he'd damned near forgotten every one. Only now could he admit that the hunger she stirred had him twisted in as many knots as her refusal to trust him with the truth. Helluva foundation to build a marriage on, he conceded grimly as he put a hand to the small of her back to guide her up the stairs.

A Filipino steward in a white jacket met them at the hatch, his seamed face creased into a smile. "Welcome aboard, Mr. Blake. I sure wouldn't have bet we'd be flying both you and Mr. Alex on honeymoons in almost the same month."

"I wouldn't have bet on it, either, Eualdo. This is my wife, Grace."

He bowed over her hand with a dignity that matched his years. "It's an honor to meet you, Ms. Grace."

"Thank you."

"If you'll follow me, I'll show you to your seats."

Blake had spent so many in-flight hours aboard the Gulfstream he'd long since come to regard it more as a necessity than a luxury. Grace's gasp when she entered the cabin reminded him not everyone would view it that way.

The interior was normally configured with high-backed, lumbar-support seats and generous workstations in addition to the galley, head and sleeping quarters. For personal or pleasure trips like this, however, the workstations were moved together to form an elegant dining area and the seats repositioned into a comfortable sitting area.

"Good grief." She gazed wide-eyed at the gleaming teak paneling and dove-gray leather. "I hope Dalton International isn't paying for all this."

"You're married to DI's chief financial officer," Blake replied dryly. "You can trust me to maintain our personal expenses separate and distinct from corporate accounts."

She flushed a little, either at the reminder that they'd just merged or at the unspoken reminder that she *wouldn't* trust him with other, more important matters.

The pink in her cheeks deepened when they passed the open door to the sleeping quarters. A quick glance inside showed the twin beds had been repositioned into a queen-size sleeper complete with down pillows, satiny sheets and a duvet with DI's logo embroidered in gold thread. Blake didn't have the least doubt that Julie and Alex had put those sheets to good use every moment they weren't in the cockpit.

Different couple, completely different circumstances. Blake and *his* bride wouldn't share that wide bed. The reality of the situation didn't block his thought of it, though. Swearing under his breath, Blake was hit with a sudden and all-too-vivid mental image of Grace stretched out with her arms raised languidly above her head, her breasts bare, her nipples turgid from his tongue and his teeth.

"I've got a bottle of Cristal on ice, Mr. Blake."

He blinked away the searing image and focused on Eualdo's weathered face.

"Shall I pour you and Ms. Grace a glass now or wait until after takeoff?"

A glance at his bride provided the answer. She had the slightly wild-eyed look of someone who was wondering just what kind of quicksand she'd stumbled into. She needed a drink or two to loosen her up. So did he. This looked to be a *long* flight.

It wound up lasting even longer than either Blake or the captain had anticipated. When they put down at a small commercial airstrip outside New York City to refuel, a thick, soupy fog rolled in off the Atlantic and delayed their departure for another two hours. The same front that produced the fog necessitated a more northerly route than originally planned.

By the time they gained enough altitude for Eualdo to serve dinner, Grace's shoulders were drooping. The steward's honey-crusted squab on a bed of wild rice and a bottle of perfectly chilled Riesling revived her enough for dessert. When darkness dropped like a stone outside the cabin windows, however, she dropped with it.

The first time her chin hit her chest, she jerked her head up and protested she was wide-awake. The second time, she gave up all attempt at pretense.

"I'm sorry." She dragged the back of her hand across her eyes. "I shouldn't have piled wine on top of champagne. I'm feeling the kick."

"Altitude probably has something to do with that."

Blake's calm reply gave no hint of his thoughts. He'd never seduced a tipsy female, but the idea was pretty damned tempting at the moment.

"It's been a long day. Why don't you go to bed?"

Her glance zinged to the rear of the cabin, shot back. "Aren't you tired?"

"Some." He put the last of his willpower into another smile. "But Eualdo's used to me working my way across the Atlantic."

"On your wedding night?"

He had no trouble interpreting the question behind the question. "He's been with Dalton International for more than a decade," he said calmly. "You don't need to worry about what he'll think. Or anyone else, for that matter."

Her glance dropped to her hands. She played with the band of diamonds, and he added getting the ring resized to his mental list of tasks to be accomplished when they returned to Oklahoma City.

"Go to bed, Grace."

Nodding, she unhooked her seat belt. Blake's hooded gaze followed her progress. When she disappeared inside the stateroom, he downed the dregs of his Riesling and reclined his seat back.

Well, Grace thought as she crawled between the sheets fifteen minutes later, she could imagine worse wedding nights. The social studies teacher in her had read enough ancient history to shudder at some of the barbaric marriage rites and rituals practiced in previous times.

In contrast, this night epitomized the ultimate in comfort and luxury. She was being whisked across an ocean in a private jet. She'd found every amenity she'd needed in the surprisingly spacious bathroom. The cotton sheets were so smooth and soft they felt like whipped cream against her skin. Two million stars winked outside the curved windows built into the bulwark. The only thing she needed to perfect the scene was a groom.

With a vengeance, all those play-wedding scenes she and her cousin had enacted as girls came back to haunt her. Hope's marriage had brought her nothing but heartache and fear. Grace's...

Oh, hell! Disgusted by her twinge of poor-me self-pity, she rolled over and thumped the pillow. She'd made her bed. She'd damned well lie in it.

Now if only she could stop with the nasty urge to march back into the main cabin and reopen negotiations. As Blake had so bluntly suggested, the sex was certainly doable. *More* than doable. The mere thought of his hard, muscled body stretched out beside her, his hands on her breasts, his mouth hot against hers, made the muscles low in Grace's belly tighten.

She clenched her legs, felt the swift pull between her thighs. Need, fierce and raw, curled through her. Her breath got shorter, faster.

This was stupid! Blake was sitting just a few yards away! Two steps to the stateroom door, one signal, silent or otherwise, and he'd join her.

Sex could be enough for now, she told herself savagely. She didn't need the shared laughter, the private smiles, the silly jokes married couples added to their storehouse of memories.

And it wasn't as though she'd arrived at this point unprepared. Teaching high school kids repeatedly reinforced basic truths, including the fact that each individual had to take responsibility for his or her protection during sex. Grace had seen too many bright, talented students' lives derailed by their biological urges. She wasn't into

one-night stands and hadn't had a serious relationship in longer than she cared to admit, but
she'd remained prepared, just in case.

So why not ease out of bed and take those two
steps to the door? Why not give the signal? She
and Blake were married, for God's sake!

She kicked off the sheet. Rolled onto a hip.
Stopped. The problem was she *wanted* the shared
smiles and silly jokes. *Needed* more than casual
sex.

"Dammit!"

Disgusted, she flopped down and hammered
the pillow again. She was a throwback. An anach-
ronism. And thoroughly, completely frustrated.

She didn't remember drifting off, but the wine
and champagne must indeed have gotten to her.
She went completely out and woke to a knock on
the stateroom door and blinding sunlight pour-
ing through the window she'd forgotten to shade.
She squinted owlishly at her watch, saw it was
the middle of the night Texas time, and had to
stifle a groan when another knock sounded.

"It's Eualdo, Ms. Grace. Mr. Blake said to let you know we're ninety minutes out."

"Okay, thanks."

"I'll serve breakfast in the main cabin when you're ready."

She emerged from the stateroom a short time later, showered and dressed in a pair of white crops and a gauzy, off-one-shoulder top in a flowery print. A chunky white bracelet added a touch of panache. She figured she would need that touch to get through her first morning-after meeting with her groom.

Blake unbuckled his seat belt and rose when she approached. Except for the discarded tie and open shirt collar, he didn't look like a man who'd sat up all night. Only when she got closer did she spot the gold bristles on his cheeks and chin.

"'Morning."

"Good morning," he answered with a smile. "Did you get any sleep?"

"I did." God! Could this be any more awkward? "How about you?"

"All I need is a shower and shave and I'll be good to go. Eualdo just brewed a fresh pot of coffee. I'll join you for breakfast as soon as I get out of the shower."

He started past her, then stopped. A rueful gleam lighting his eyes, he brushed a knuckle across her cheek.

"We'll figure this out, Grace. We just need to give it time."

Time, she repeated silently as the Gulfstream swooped low over a dazzling turquoise sea in preparation for landing. Despite her inner agitation, the sweeping view of the Mediterranean enchanted her.

So did the balmy tropical climate that greeted them. Grace had watched several movies and travel specials featuring the south of France. She'd also read a good number of books with the same setting, most recently a Dan Brown–type thriller that had the protagonists searching for a long-lost fragment of the Jesus's cross at the popes' sprawling palace in Avignon. None of the books or movies or travelogues prepared her for Provence's cloudless skies and brilliant sunshine, however. She held up a hand to block the rays as she deplaned, breathing in the briny tang of the sea that surrounded the Marseille airport.

A driver was waiting at the small aircraft terminal with a sporty red convertible. After he'd stashed their bags in the trunk, he made a polite inquiry in French. Blake responded with a smile and a nod.

"Oui."

"C'est bien. Bon voyage."

Grace glanced at him curiously as he slid behind the wheel. "You speak French?"

"Not according to Cecile."

Right. Cecile. The chef who owned the restaurant where Alex and Julie had hosted their rehearsal dinner. The gorgeous, long-legged chef who'd draped herself all over Blake. That display of Gallic exuberance hadn't bothered Grace at the time. Much. It did now. With some effort, she squashed the memory and settled into the convertible.

Blake got behind the wheel. He'd changed into khakis and a fresh shirt and hooked a pair of aviator sunglasses on his shirt pocket.

"Just out of curiosity," she commented as he slipped on the glasses, "where are we going?"

"Saint-Rémy-de-Provence. It's a small town about an hour north of here." A smile played at the corners of his mouth. "A nationwide transportation strike stranded Mother there during one of her antique-hunting trips about five years ago. She used the downtime to buy a crumbling villa and turn it into a vacation resort for top-performing DI employees and their families."

Grace had to grin. That sounded just like her employer. Correction, her mother-in-law. Delilah Dalton possessed more energy and drive than any six people her age.

"The place was occupied most recently by DI's top three welding teams and their families," he added casually. "But Madame LeBlanc indicated we'll have it to ourselves for the next two weeks."

Not so casually, Grace's heart thumped hard against her ribs. The combustible mix of lust and longing she'd had to battle last night had been bad enough. How the heck was she going to get through the next two weeks? Alone. With Blake.

Under the hot Provencal sun and starry, starry nights.

Slowly she sank into her seat.

Six

A little over an hour later Blake turned off the autoroute onto a two-lane road shaded by towering sycamores. Their branches met overhead to form a green tunnel that stretched for miles. The rocky pinnacles of the Alpilles thrust out of the earth to the left of the road. Sun-drenched vineyards and olive groves rolled out on the right, flashing through the sycamores' white, scaly trunks like a DVD run in fast-forward.

As delightful as the approach to Saint-Rémy was, the town itself enchanted Grace even more. Eighteenth-century mansions that Blake called *hôtels* lined the busy street encircling the town proper. Dolphins spouted in a fountain marking one quadrant of the circle, stone goddesses poured water from urns at another. In the pedestrians-only heart of the town, Grace caught glimpses of narrow lanes crammed with shops and open-air restaurants that invited patrons to sit and sip a cappuccino.

Blake noticed her craning her neck to peer down the intriguing alleyways. "We'll have lunch in town," he promised.

"I'd like that."

She studied her groom as he negotiated the busy street. He fit perfectly against this elegant eighteenth-century backdrop, Grace decided. The corporate executive had shed his suit and tie but not his sophistication. Sunlight glinted on the sleek watch banding his wrist and the light dusting of golden hair on his forearm. The aviator sunglasses and hand-tailored shirt left open at the neck to show the tanned column of his throat only added to the image.

"Madame LeBlanc will meet us at Hôtel des Elmes," he added as he skillfully wove through pedestrians, tourists and traffic.

She took a stab at a translation. "The Elms?"

"The Elms," he confirmed. "It used to be called the Hôtel Saint Jacques. Legend has it that the original owner claimed to have invented, or at least improved on, the scallop dish named in Saint James's honor."

Grace had to think for a moment. "Aha! Coquilles St. Jacques!"

"Right. You'll be pleased to know the current chef at the *hôtel* has followed in his predecessors' footsteps. Auguste's scallops au gratin will make you think you hear heavenly choirs."

The easy banter took them up to a pair of tall, wrought-iron gates left open in anticipation of their arrival. Once inside, Grace understood instantly the inspiration for the villa's new designation. Majestic elms that must have been planted more than a century ago formed a graceful arch above a crushed-stone drive. The curving drive wound through landscaped grounds dotted with statuary and vine-shaded arbors, then ended in a circle dominated by a twenty-foot fountain featuring bronze steeds spouting arcs of silvery water.

And looming beyond the fountain was a masterpiece in mellowed gray stone. The Hôtel des Elmes consisted of a three-story central wing, with two-story wings on each side. Wisteria vines softened its elaborate stone facade, drooping showy purple blossoms from wrought-iron trellises. Grace breathed in the purple blossoms' spicy vanilla scent as Blake braked to a stop.

The front door opened before he'd killed the engine. The woman who emerged fit Grace's mental image of the quintessential older French female—slender, charming, impossibly chic in silky black slacks and a cool linen blouse.

"Bienvenue à Saint-Rémy, Monsieur Blake."

"It's good to be back," he replied in English.

After the obligatory cheek kissing, he introduced Grace. She must have been getting used to being presented as his wife. She barely squirmed when Madame LeBlanc grasped both her hands and offered a profuse welcome.

"I am most happy to meet you." Madame's smile took a roguish tilt. "Delilah has long despaired of getting her so-handsome sons to the altar. One can only imagine how thrilled she must be that Alex and Blake have taken brides within a month of each other. *Quelle romantique!*"

"Yes, well…"

Blake's arm slid around Grace's waist. *"Trés romantique."*

His casual comment fed the fantasy of a honeymoon couple. Madame LeBlanc sighed her approval and handed him a set of tagged keys.

"As you instructed, the staff will not report until tomorrow, but Auguste has prepared several dishes should you wish them. They need only to be reheated. And the upstairs maid has made up the bed in the Green Suite and left for the rest of the day. You will not be disturbed."

"Merci."

If the villa's grounds and exquisite eighteenth-century exterior evoked visions of aristocrats in silks and powered wigs, the interior had obviously been retrofitted for twenty-first-century visitors. Grace spotted high-tech security cameras above the doors and an alarm panel just inside the entryway that looked as if it would take an MIT grad to program. The brass-accented elevator tucked discreetly behind a screen of potted palms was also a modern addition.

While Grace peeked around, Blake carried in their few bags and deposited them in the marbled foyer. "Would you like the ten-cent tour, or would you rather go upstairs and rest for a while first?"

"The tour, please! Unless…" Guilt tripped her. "I'm sorry. I zoned out on the plane, but you didn't. You're probably aching for bed."

Something shifted in his face. A mere ripple of skin across muscle and bone. Grace didn't have time to interpret the odd look before he masked it.

"I'm good." He made an exaggerated bow and swept an arm toward the central hall. "This way, madame."

Grace soon lost count of the downstairs rooms. There was the petite salon, the grand salon, the music room, the library, the card room, an exquisitely mirrored ballroom and several banquet and eating areas in addition to the kitchens and downstairs powder rooms. Each contained a mix of antiques and ultramodern conveniences cleverly integrated into an elegant yet inviting whole.

Even the painted porcelain sinks in the powder rooms evoked an eighteenth-century feel, and the copper-and-spice-filled kitchen could accommodate cooks of all ages and eras.

The pool house with its marble columns and bougainvillea-draped pergola was a Greek fantasy come to life. The shimmering turquoise water in the pool made Grace itch to shed her clothes on the spot and dive in. But when they went back inside again and started for the stairs to the second floor, it was the painting of deep purple irises displayed in a lighted alcove that stopped her dead.

"Ooooh!" Grace was no art expert, but even she could recognize a Van Gogh when it smacked her between the eyes. "I have a poster of this same painting in my bedroom."

Blake paused behind her. "That's one of my mother's favorites, too. She donated the original to the Smithsonian's Museum of Modern Art but had this copy commissioned for the villa."

He was only an inch or two from her shoulder. So close she felt his breath wash warm and soft against her ear. The sensation zinged down her spine and stirred a reaction that almost made her miss Blake's next comment.

"This is one of the more than one hundred and fifty paintings Van Gogh painted during his year in Saint-Rémy. There's a walking tour that shows the various scenes he incorporated into his works. We can take it if you like."

"I would!"

The possibility of viewing sunflowers and olive groves through the eyes of one of the world's greatest artists tantalized Grace. Almost as much as the idea of viewing them with Blake.

Hard on that came the realization that she had no clue if her new husband was the least bit interested in impressionist art. Or what kind of music he preferred. Or how he spent his downtime when he wasn't doing his executive/corporate lawyer thing. She'd known him such a short time. And during those weeks he, his twin and his indomitable parent had focused exclusively on Molly and the hunt for the baby's mother.

Could be this enforced honeymoon wasn't such a bad idea after all. The main participants in every partnership, even a marriage of conve-

nience, needed to establish a working relationship. Maybe Delilah had their best interests at
heart when she'd arranged this getaway.

Maybe. It was hard to tell what really went on
in the woman's Machiavellian mind. Withholding
judgment, Grace accompanied Blake on a tour
of the second story. He pointed out several fully
contained guest suites, two additional salons,
a reading room, even a video game room for
the children of the Dalton employees and other
guests who stayed at the *hôtel.* At the end of the
hall, he opened a set of double doors fitted with
gold-plated latches.

"This is the master suite." His mouth took a
wry tilt. "Otherwise known as the Green Suite."

Grace could certainly see why! Awed, she let
her gaze travel from floor-to-ceiling silk wall
panels to elegantly looped drapes to the thick
duvet and dozens of tasseled pillows mounded
on the four-poster bed. They were all done in a
shimmering, iridescent brocade that shaded from
moss-green to dark jade depending on the angle
of the light streaming through the French doors.
The bed itself was inlaid mahogany chased with

gold. *Lots* of gold. So were the bombe chests and marble-topped tables scattered throughout the suite.

"Wow!" Mesmerized by the opulence, she spun in a slow circle. "This looks like Louis XV might have slept here."

"There's no record the king ever made it down," Blake returned with a grin, "but one of his mistresses reportedly entertained another of her lovers here on the sly."

Grace couldn't decide which hit with more of a wallop, that quick grin or the instant and totally erotic image his comment stirred. As vividly as any painting, she could picture a woman in white silk stockings, ribboned garters and an unlaced corset lolling against the four-poster's mounds of pillows. A bare-chested courtier with Blake Dalton's guinea-gold hair leaned over her. His blue eyes glinted with wicked promise as he slowly slid one of her garters from her thigh to her knee to her…

"…the adjoining suite."

Blinking, she zoomed out of the eighteenth century. "Sorry. I was, uh, thinking of powdered wigs and silk knee breeches. What did you say?"

"I said I'll be in the adjoining suite."

The last of the delicious image fizzled as Grace watched her husband open a connecting door. The bedroom beyond wasn't as large or as decadent as that of the Green Suite, but it did boast another four-poster and a marble fireplace big enough to roast an ox.

"It's almost noon Saint-Rémy time," Blake said after a quick glance at his watch. "If you're not too jet-lagged, we could reconvene in a half hour and walk into town for lunch."

"That works for me."

Calling herself an idiot for staring at the door long after it closed behind him, Grace extracted her toiletries from her tote bag and carried them into a bathroom fit for a queen. Or at least a royal mistress.

Maybe it was the glorious sun that sucked away her sense of awkwardness. Or the lazy, protracted lunch she and Blake shared at a dime-size table cornered next to a bubbling fountain. Or the two glasses of perfectly chilled rosé produced by a vineyard right outside Saint-Rémy.

Then again, it might have been Blake's obvious efforts to keep the conversation light and non-controversial. He made no reference to the circumstances of their marriage or Grace's adamant refusal to betray her cousin's trust. As a consequence, she felt herself relaxing for the first time in longer than she could remember.

The still-raw ache of her cousin's death shifted to a corner of her heart. Jack Petrie, Oklahoma City, even Molly moved off center stage. Not completely, and certainly not for long. Yet these hours in the sun provided a hiatus from the worry she'd carted around for so many months. That was the only excuse she could come up with later for the stupidity that followed.

It happened during the walk back to their *hôtel*. Blake indulged her with a stroll through the town's pedestrian-only center, stopping repeatedly while she oooh'ed and aaaah'ed over shop windows displaying Provence's wares. One window was filled with colorful baskets containing every imaginable spice and herb. Another specialized in soaps and scented oils. *Hundreds* of soaps and oils. Delighted, Grace went inside and sniffed at products made from apple pear, lemon, peony, vanilla, honey almond and, of course, lavender. A dazzling display of stoppered vials offered bath oils and lotions in a rainbow of hues.

The clerk obviously knew her business. She sized up the diamonds circling Grace's finger in a single glance. With a knowing look, she produced a cut-crystal vial from a shelf behind the counter.

"Madame must try this. It is a special blend made only for our shop."

When she removed the stopper, an exquisitely delicate aroma drifted across the counter. Lavender and something else that Grace couldn't quite identify.

"The perfumers extract oil from the buds before they blossom. The fragrance is light, *oui?* So very light and yet, how do you say? So *sensuelle.*"

She waved the stopper in the air to release more of its bouquet. Grace leaned forward, breathing deeply. She knew then that whatever else happened in this marriage, she would always associate the scent of lavender with sunshine and brilliant skies and the smile crinkling the skin at the corners of Blake's eyes as he watched her sniffing the air.

He didn't remain an observer for long. Sensing a sale, the shopkeeper dipped the stopper again. "Here, *monsieur,* you must dab some on your wife's wrist. The oil takes on a richer tone when applied to the skin."

With a good-natured nod, Blake took the stopper in one hand and reached for Grace's wrist with the other. His hold was loose, easy. As light as it was, though, the touch sent a ripple of pleasure along her nerves. The ripple swelled to a tidal wave when he raised her arm to a mere inch or so from his nose.

"She's right," he murmured. The blue in his eyes deepened as he caught Grace's gaze. "The warmth of your skin deepens the scent."

Warmth? Ha! She'd passed mere warmth the moment his fingers circled her wrist. And if he kept looking at her like that, she suspected she would spontaneously combust in the next five seconds.

Thankfully, the shop clerk claimed his attention. The distraction proved only temporary, however. Eager for a sale, the woman urged another test.

"Dab a little dab behind your wife's ear, *monsieur.* It is of all places the most seductive."

Grace's internal alarm went off like a klaxon. Every scrap of common sense she possessed urged her to decline the second sample. The sun and the wine and this man's touch were bringing her too close to the melting point. So she was damned if she knew why she just stood there and let Blake brush aside her hair.

The crystal stopper was cool and damp against the skin just below her earlobe. An instant later, her husband's breath seared that same patch of skin. Their only physical contact point was the hand caging back her hair. If the shock that went though her was any indication, however, they might have been locked together at chest and hip and thigh. Thoroughly shaken, Grace took a step back.

The abrupt move brought Blake's head up with a snap. He didn't need to see the confusion on his wife's face to know he'd crossed the line.

The line he'd been stupid enough to draw! He was the one who'd assured her they would work things out. He'd spouted that inane drivel about giving their arrangement time.

To hell with waiting. He ached to drag Grace out of the shop, hustle her back to The Elms and strip her down to the warm, perfumed flesh that was sending his senses into dangerous overload.

"Monsieur?"

The shop clerk's voice cut through his red haze. Before Blake could bring the woman into focus, he had to exercise the iron will that allowed him to appear calm before judges and juries.

She finally appeared, smiling and eager. "Do you wish to purchase a vial for your so-lovely wife?"

God, yes!

At his nod, she whipped out a sales slip. "Do you stay here in Saint-Rémy?"

He knew his address would up the asking price

by at least half but was beyond caring. "We're at Hôtel des Elmes."

Her glance sharpened. "Ahhh. I recognize you now. You came to Saint-Rémy last year, *oui*? With... Er..." She broke off, then recovered after an infinitesimal pause. "With your so very charming mother."

Riiiight. Blake seriously doubted his twin had timed a visit to the villa to coincide with one of their mother's protracted stays. Alex and Delilah were both obviously well-known in town, however, so he didn't bother to correct the clerk's misconception.

"We'll take a bottle of that scent."

Beaming, she rattled off the price for a three-ounce bottle. He was reaching for his money clip when Grace gave a strangled gasp.

"Did you say two hundred euros?"

"*Oui,* madame."

"Two *hundred* euros?"

"*Oui.*"

"That's like..."

Blake paused in the act of peeling off several euro notes while she did the mental math.

"Good grief! That's almost three hundred dollars U.S." Horrified, she closed her hand over his. "That's too much."

A pained look crossed the salesclerk's face. "You will not find a more distinctive or more delicate scent in all Provence. And…"

Her glance cut to Blake. When she turned back to Grace, a conspiratorial smile tilted her lips.

"If I may say so, madame, your husband does not purchase this fragrance for you. He is the one who will detect its essence on your skin. If it pleases him…"

Her shoulders lifted in that most Gallic of all gestures, and Grace could only watch helplessly as Blake dropped the euro notes on the counter.

<u>Seven</u>

Even with Grace's seductive scent delivering a broadside every time Blake turned his head or leaned toward her, he didn't plan what happened when they returned to the villa. His conscience would always remain clear on that point. When he suggested a swim, his only intent was to continue the easy camaraderie established during lunch.

What he *hadn't* anticipated was the kick to his gut when Grace joined him poolside and slipped off her terry cloth cover-up. He'd already done a half dozen laps but wasn't the least winded until the sight of her slender, seductive curves sucked the air from his lungs.

"How's the water?"

Blake tried to untangle his tongue. Damned thing felt like it was wrapped in cotton wool. "Cool at first," he got out after an epic struggle. "Not so bad once you're in."

Oh, for God's sake! Her suit was a poppy-colored one-piece that covered more than it revealed. Yet he was damned if he could stop his gaze from devouring the slopes of her breasts when she bent to deposit her towel on the lounger. That unexpected jolt was followed by another when she turned to dip a toe in the water and gave him an unimpeded view of the curve of her bottom cheeks.

"Yikes!" She jerked her foot back with a yelp and zinged him an indignant look. "You think this is *cool?* What's your definition of *cold?* Minus forty?"

He grinned and tread water as she dipped another cautious toe. Her face screwed into a grimace. She inched down a step, her shoulders hunched almost to her ears. Eased onto the next step. The water swirled around her calves, her thighs.

"Coward," he teased.

She took another tentative step, and his grin slipped. The water lapped the lower edge of her suit. The bright red material dampened at the apex of her thighs and provided a throat-closing outline of what lay beneath.

"Oh, hell."

He barely heard her mutter of self-disgust. Or felt the splash when she gathered her courage and flopped all the way in. She bobbed up a moment later, her hair a sleek waterfall of pale gold. Sparkling drops beaded her lashes. Laughter lit her eyes.

Something inside Blake shifted. He didn't see the woman who'd lied to him and his family by omission, or the conspirator who'd withheld crucial information about the mother of his child. There were no shadows haunting the eyes of this laughing, splashing water sprite. For the moment at least, no memories constrained her simple pleasure. It was a glimpse of the woman Grace must have been before she took on the burden of her cousin's secrets. An even more tantalizing hint of the woman who might reemerge if and when she shed that burden.

Without conscious thought, Blake realigned his priorities. Convincing his bride to trust him remained his primary goal. Getting her into bed ran a close second. But keeping that carefree laughter in her eyes was fast elbowing its way up close to the top of the list.

"All right," she gasped, dancing on her toes. "I'm in. When does it get to 'not so bad'?"

"Do a couple laps. You'll warm up quick enough."

She made a face but took his suggestion. He rolled into an easy breaststroke and kept pace with her. She had a smooth, clean stroke, he noted with approval, a nice kick. Two laps turned into three, then four. Or what would have been four.

She made the turn, pushed off the wall at an angle and submarined into him. They went under in a tangle of arms and legs. She came up sputtering. He came up with his bride plastered against his chest.

"Sorry!"

Blinking the water out of her eyes, she clung to him. They were at the deep end, in well over their heads. Literally, Blake thought, as her thighs scissored between his. Maybe figuratively.

Hell, there was no maybe about it. He wanted her with a raw need he didn't try to analyze. She must have seen it in his face, felt his muscles tighten under her slick, slippery hands. She looked up at him with a question in her eyes.

"According to our contract," he got out on a near rasp, "any and all physical contact must be by mutual consent. If you don't want this to go any further, you'd better say so now."

After a pause that just about ripped out Blake's guts, she clamped her lips shut and matched him look for look. With another growl, he claimed her mouth.

The kiss was swift and hot and hungry. If he'd interpreted her silence wrong, if she'd tried to push away, Blake would've released her. He was almost sure of that. She didn't, thank God, and he threw off every vestige of restraint.

They went under again, mouths and bodies fused. When they resurfaced, Blake kept her pinned, gave two swift kicks and took them to the wall. He flattened her against the tiles, using one hand to hold them both up while he attacked one strap of her suit with the other. The skin of her shoulder was soft and cool and slick. The mingled scents of lavender and chlorine acted like a spur, turning hunger into greed.

He switched hands, yanked down the other strap. She was as anxious now to shuck her bathing suit as he was to get her out of it. A wiggle, a shimmy, a kick, and it was gone. His followed two heartbeats later.

Her breast fit perfectly in his palm. The flesh was firm and smooth, the tip already stiff from the cold water. He rolled the nipple between his thumb and forefinger and damned near lost it when she arched her back to give him access to her other breast. He hiked her up a few inches, devouring her with teeth and tongue while he slicked his hand down her belly.

"Oh, God!"

Moaning, Grace threw her head back. She'd agreed to this. Had spent more than a few hours tossing around the idea of casual sex with this man. But this—this was nowhere near casual! Blake's mouth scorched her breasts, her shoulder, her throat. And her heart almost jumped out of her chest when he curved his fingers over her mound and parted her crease. She moaned again as he thrust into her and, to her utter mortification, exploded.

The orgasm ripped through her. She rode it blindly, mindlessly, until the spasms died and she flopped like a wet rag doll against his chest.

The thunder in her ears didn't subside. If anything, it grew louder. Only gradually did Grace realize that was Blake's heart tattooing against her ear. Gathering her shattered senses, she raised her head and curved her lips.

The skin at the corners of his blues eyes crinkled as he started to return her smile. Then she wrapped her legs around his hips and his expression froze. Slowly, sensually, she lifted her hips, positioning herself.

"Wait," he got out on a strangled grunt. "We need to take this inside."

"Why?"

"Protection. You need pro…" He broke off, hissing as she angled her hips. "Grace…"

He didn't say it, but she guessed he was thinking of Molly. She certainly was.

"It's okay," she said, breathless and urgent. "I'm covered."

He reacted to that bit of news with gratifying speed. Planting a foot against the tiles, he propelled them toward the shallow end. The sparkling water cascaded over his shoulders and chest as he took a wide stance and hefted her bottom with both palms.

A fresh wave of desire coiled deep in Grace's belly. Eager to give him some of the explosive pleasure he'd given her, she wrapped her legs around his waist. She didn't want slow. Didn't want gentle. When he thrust into her, she slapped her hips into his and clenched every muscle in her body.

He held out longer than she had. Much longer. Grace was close to losing control again when his fingers dug into her bottom cheeks. He went rigid and jammed her against him at an angle that put exquisite, unbearable pressure right where she wanted it the most. With a ragged groan, she arched into another shuddering, shattering climax. This time she took him with her.

Jet lag, a lack of sleep and the most intense sex he'd ever had combined to plow into Blake like an Abrams tank. He remembered helping Grace out of the water and savoring the view before she wrapped herself in one of the villa's blue-and-white-striped pool towels. He vaguely recalled diving back in to retrieve their bathing suits. He wasn't sure whether he'd suggested they stretch out in one of the loungers inside the vine-covered pergola, or she had. But the next time he opened his eyes, the sun had disappeared and hundreds of tiny white lights made a fairyland of the pool area.

He sat up, blinking, and scraped a hand across a sandpaper chin. The movement drew the attention of the woman on the lounger beside his.

"What time is it?" he asked, his voice still thick with sleep.

"I'm not sure. My internal clock is still set to Texas time." She glanced at the canopy of stars outside the pergola. "I'm guessing it's probably nine or nine-thirty."

Blake winced. Great! Absolutely great! Nothing demonstrated a man's virility like taking four or five hours to recharge after sex.

"Sorry I passed out on you."

"No problem." His obvious chagrin had a smile hovering at the corners of her mouth. "I napped, too."

Not for long, apparently. She'd used some of the time he was out cold to change into khaki shorts and a scoop-necked T-shirt. Her hair looked freshly washed, its shining length caught up in a plastic clip.

"Have you eaten?"

"I was waiting for you."

He was still in the swim trunks he'd brought up from the pool. They were dry now and rode low on his hips as he pushed off the lounger and reached out to help her up.

"Let's go raid the kitchen."

The hesitation before she took his hand was so brief he might have imagined it. He couldn't miss the constraint that kept her silent, though, once they'd settled in high-backed wrought-iron stools at the kitchen's monster, green-tiled island. As Madame LeBlanc had indicated, the chef had left a gourmand's dream of sumptuous choices in the fridge and on the counters. Grace opted for a bowl of cold, spicy gazpacho and a chunk of bread torn from one of the long, crusty baguettes poking out of a wire basket. Blake poured them both a glass of light, fruity chardonnay before heaping his plate with salad Niçoise and a man-size wedge of asparagus-and-goat-cheese quiche warmed in the microwave.

He forked down several bites of salad, savoring its red, ripe tomatoes and anchovies, eyeing Grace as she played with her bread, waiting for her to break the small silence. He had a good idea what was behind her sudden constraint. Morning-after nerves, or in this case, evening-after.

She validated his guess a few moments later. Drawing in a deep breath, she tackled the thorny subject head-on. "About what happened in the pool…"

He sensed what was coming and wasn't about to make it easy for her. "What about it?"

"I know we put the possibility of sex on the table when we negotiated this, uh, partnership."

"But?"

She looked down, crumbled her bread, met his gaze again. "But things just spun out of control. I'm as much to blame as you are," she added quickly. "Now that I've had time to think, though, it was too quick, Blake. Too fast."

"We'll take it slower next time."

The solemn promise almost won a smile.

"I *meant* it was too soon. I'm still trying to adjust to this whole marriage business."

"I know." Serious now, he laid down his fork. "But let's clarify one matter. Things didn't just spin out of control. I wanted you, Grace."

Color tinted her cheeks. "I'll concede that point, counselor. And it was obvious I wanted you."

"I understand this is an adjustment period for you, however. For both of us. We've a lot yet to learn about each other."

The deliberate reference to her hoard of secrets brought her chin up. "Exactly. Which is why we should avoid a repetition of what happened this afternoon until you're comfortable with who I am and vice versa."

What the hell would it take to get her to trust him? Irritation put a bite in Blake's voice. "So we just revert back to cool and polite? You think it'll be that easy?"

"No," she admitted, "but necessary if this arrangement of ours is going to work."

He swallowed the bitter aftertaste of anchovies and frustration. "All right. We'll take hot, wild sex off the agenda. For now."

Grace spent the second night of her honeymoon the same way she had her first, restless and conflicted and alone.

While moonlight streamed through windows left open to a soft night breeze, she punched the mounded pillow and replayed the scene in the kitchen. She'd been right to put the brakes on. The way she'd flamed in Blake's arms, lost every ounce of rational thought... She'd never gone so mindless with hunger before. Never craved a man's touch and the wild sensation of his hard, sculpted body crushing hers.

She'd had time to think while Blake dozed this afternoon, and the fact that she'd abandoned herself so completely had shaken her. Still shook her! She'd witnessed firsthand the misery her cousin endured, for God's sake. Had helped Anne run, hide, struggle painfully to regain her confidence and self-respect. Grace couldn't just throw off the brutal burden of those months and years. Nor could she dump it on Blake's broad, willing shoulders—much as she ached to.

No, she was right to pull back. Revert to cool and polite, to use his phrase. They both needed time to adjust to this awkward marriage before they took the next step. Whatever the heck that was.

It took a severe exercise of will, but she managed to block the mental image of Blake pinning her to the tiles and drop into sleep.

She remained firm in her resolve to back things up a step when she went down for breakfast the next morning.

The villa's staff had obviously reported for duty. The heavenly scent of fresh-baked bread wafted from the direction of the kitchen, and a maid in a pale blue uniform wielded a feather duster like a baton at the foot of the stairs. Her eyes lit with curiosity and a friendly welcome when she spotted Grace.

"*Bonjour,* Madame Dalton."

"*Bonjour.*"

That much Grace could manage. The quick spate that followed had her offering an apology.

"I'm sorry. I don't speak French."

"Ah, *excusez-moi.* I am Marie. The downstairs maid, yes? I am most happy to meet you."

"Thank you. It's nice to meet you, too."

She hesitated, not exactly embarrassed but not real eager to admit she didn't have a clue where her husband of two days might be. Luckily, Blake had primed the staff with the necessary information.

"Monsieur Dalton said to tell you that he takes coffee on the east terrace," Marie informed her cheerfully. "He waits for you to join him for breakfast."

"And the east terrace is...?"

"Just there, madame." She aimed the feather duster. "Through the petite salon."

"Thanks."

She crossed the salon's exquisitely thick carpet and made for a set of open French doors that gave onto a flagstone terrace enclosed by ivy-drenched stone walls. A white wrought-iron table held a silver coffee service and a basket of brioche. Blake held his Blackberry and was working the keyboard one-handed while he sipped from a gold-rimmed china cup with the other.

Grace stopped just inside the French doors to drag in several deep breaths. She needed them. The sight of her husband in the clear, shimmering light of a Provencal morning was something to behold. A stray sunbeam snuck through the elms shading the patio to gild his hair. His crisp blue shirt was open at the neck and rolled at the cuffs. He looked calm and collected and too gorgeous for words, dammit!

She sucked in another breath and stepped out onto the patio. "Good morning."

He set down both his coffee cup and the Blackberry and rose.

"Good morning." The greeting was as courteous and impersonal as his smile. "Did you sleep well?"

Right. Okay. This was how she wanted it. What she'd insisted on.

"Very well," she lied. "You?"

"As well as could be expected after yesterday afternoon."

When she flashed a warning look, he shed his polite mask and hooked a brow.

"I zoned out for a good four hours on that lounge chair," he reminded her. "As a consequence, I didn't need much sleep last night."

And if she bought that one, Blake thought sardonically, he had several more he could sell her.

He didn't have to sell them. The swift way she broke eye contact told him she suspected he was stretching the truth until it damned near screamed.

She had to know she'd kept him awake most of the night. She, and her absurd insistence they ignore the wildfire they'd sparked yesterday. As if they could. The heat of it still singed Blake's mind and burned in his gut.

In the small hours of the night he'd called himself every kind of an idiot for agreeing to this farcical facade. It made even less sense in the bright light of morning. They couldn't shove yesterday in a box, stick it on the closet shelf and pretend it never happened. Yet he *had* agreed, and now he was stuck with it.

It didn't improve his mood to discover she'd dabbed on some of the perfumed oil he'd bought her yesterday. The provocative scent tugged at his senses as he pulled out one of the heavy wrought-iron chairs for her.

"Why don't you pour yourself some coffee and I'll tell Auguste we're ready for... Ah, here he is."

At first glance few people would tag the individual who appeared in the open French doors as a graduate of Le Cordon Bleu and two-time winner of the *Coupe du Monde de la Patisserie*— the World Cup of pastry. He sported stooped shoulders, sparse gray hair and a hound-dog face with dewlaps that hung in mournful folds. If he'd cracked a smile anytime in the past two years, Blake sure hadn't seen it.

The great Auguste had been retired for a decade and, according to Delilah, going out of his gourd with boredom when she'd hunted him down. After subjecting the poor man to the full force of her personality, she'd convinced him to take over the kitchen of Hôtel des Elmes.

Blake had made his way to the kitchen earlier to say hello. He now introduced the chef to Grace. Auguste bowed over her hand and greeted her in tones of infinite sadness.

"I welcome you to Saint-Rémy."

Gulping, she threw Blake a what-in-the-world-did-I-do look? He stepped in smoothly.

"I've told Grace about your scallops au gratin, Auguste. Perhaps you'll prepare them for us one evening."

"But of course." He heaved a long-suffering sigh and turned his doleful gaze back to Grace. "Tonight, if you wish it, madame."

"That would be wonderful. Thank you."

"And now I shall prepare the eggs Benedict for you and *monsieur,* yes?"

"Er, yes. Please."

He bowed again and retreated, shoulders drooping. Grace followed his exit with awed eyes.

"Did someone close to him just die?" she whispered to Blake.

The question broke the ice that had crusted between them. Laughing, Blake went back to his
own seat.

"Not that I know of. In fact, you're seeing him
in one of his more cheerful moods."

"Riiight."

With a doubtful glance at the French doors, she
spread her napkin across her lap. He waited until
she'd filled a cup with rich, dark brew to offer
the basket of fresh-baked brioche.

"We've got dinner taken care of," he said as
she slathered on butter and thick strawberry jam.
"What would you like to do until then?"

She sent him a quick look, saw he hadn't packed
some hidden meaning into the suggestion, and relaxed into her first genuine smile of the morning.

"You mentioned a Van Gogh trail. I'd love to
explore that, if you're up for it."

Resolutely, Blake suppressed the memory of his
mother ruthlessly dragging Alex and him along

every step of the route commemorating Saint-Rémy's most famous artist.

"I'm up for it."

Eight

Grace couldn't have asked for a more perfect day to explore. Sometime while they'd been over the Atlantic, August had rolled into September. The absolute best time to enjoy Provence's balmy breezes and dazzling sunshine, Blake assured her as the sporty red convertible crunched down the front drive. It was still warm enough for her to be glad she'd opted for linen slacks and a cap-sleeved black T-shirt with I ♥ Texas picked out in sparkly rhinestones. She'd caught her hair back in a similarly adorned ball cap to keep the ends from whipping her face.

Blake hadn't bothered with a hat, but his mirrored aviation sunglasses protected his eyes from the glare. With his blue shirt open at the neck and the cuffs rolled up on his forearms, he looked cool and comfortable and too damned sexy for his own or Grace's good.

"I wasn't sure how much you know about Vincent van Gogh," he said with a sideways glance, "so I printed off a short bio while you were getting ready."

"Thanks." She gratefully accepted the folded page he pulled out of his shirt pocket. "I went to a traveling exhibit at the San Antonio Museum of Art that featured several of his sketches a few years ago. I don't know much about the man himself, though, except that he was Dutch and disturbed enough to cut off his left ear."

"He was certainly disturbed, but there's some dispute over whether he deliberately hacked off his ear or lost it in the scuffle when he went after his pal Gauguin with a straight razor."

While Blake navigated shaded streets toward the outskirts of Saint-Rémy, Grace absorbed the details in the life of the brilliant, tormented artist who killed himself at the age of thirty-seven.

"It says here Van Gogh only sold one painting during his lifetime and died thinking himself a failure. How sad."

"Very sad," Blake agreed.

"Especially since his self-portrait is listed here as one of the ten most expensive paintings ever sold," Grace read, her eyes widening. "It went for $71 million in 1998."

"Which would equate to about $90 million today, adjusted for inflation."

"Good grief!"

She couldn't imagine paying that kind of money for anything short of a supersonic jet transport. Then she remembered the painting of the irises at the villa, and Blake's casual comment that his mother had donated the original to the Smithsonian.

She'd known the Daltons operated in a rarified financial atmosphere, of course. She'd lived in Delilah's rambling Oklahoma City mansion for several months and assisted her with some of her pet charity projects. She'd also picked up bits and pieces about the various megadeals Alex and Blake had in the works at DI. And she'd certainly gotten a firsthand taste of the luxury she'd married into during the flight across the Atlantic and at the Hôtel des Elmes. But for some reason the idea of forking over eighty or ninety million for a painting made it all seem surreal.

Her glance dropped to the diamonds banding her finger. They were certainly real enough. A whole lot more real than the union they supposedly symbolized. Although yesterday, at the pool…

No! Better not go there! She'd just get all confused and conflicted again. Best just to enjoy the sun and the company of the intriguing man she'd married.

A flash of white diverted her attention to the right side of the road. Eyes popping, she stared at a massive arch and white marble tower spearing up toward the sky. "What are those?"

"They're called *Les Antiques*. They're the most visible remnants of the Roman town of Glanum that once occupied this site. The rest of the ruins are a little farther down the road. We'll save exploring them for another day."

He turned left instead of right and drove down

a tree-shaded lane bordered on one side by a vacant field and on the other by tall cypresses and the twisted trunks of an olive grove. Beyond the grove the rocky spine of the Alpilles slashed across the horizon.

"Here we are."

"Here," Grace discovered, was the Saint-Paul de Mausole Asylum, which Van Gogh had voluntarily entered in May 1889. Behind its ivy-covered gray stone walls she glimpsed a church tower and a two- or three-story rectangular building.

"Saint-Paul's was originally an Augustine monastery," Blake explained as he maneuvered into a parking space next to two tour buses. "Built in the eleventh or twelfth century, I think. It was converted to an asylum in the 1800s and is still used as a psychiatric hospital. The hospital is off-limits, of course, but the church, the cloister and the rooms where Van Gogh lived and painted are open to the public."

A very interested public, it turned out. The tour buses had evidently just disgorged their passengers. Guides shepherded their charges through the gates and up to the ticket booth. After the chattering tourists clicked through the turnstile single file, Blake paid for two entries and picked up an informational brochure but caught Grace's elbow once they'd passed through the turnstile.

"Let them get a little way ahead. You'll want to experience some of the tranquility Van Gogh did when he was allowed outside to paint."

She had no problem dawdling. The path leading to the church and other buildings was long and shady and lined on both sides by glossy rhododendron and colorful flowers. Adding to her delight, plaques spaced along the walk highlighted a particular view and contrasted it with Van Gogh's interpretation of that same scene.

A depiction of one of his famous sunflower paintings was displayed above a row of almost identical bright yellow flowers nodding in the sun. A low point in the wall provided a sweeping view of silvery-leafed olive trees dominated by the razor-backed mountain peaks in the distance. Van Gogh's version of that scene was done with his signature intense colors and short, bold brushstrokes. Fascinated, Grace stood before the plaque and glanced repeatedly from the trees' gnarled, twisted trunks to the artist's interpretation.

"This is amazing!" she breathed. "It's like stepping into a painting and seeing everything that went into it through different eyes."

She lingered at that plaque for several moments before meandering down the shady path to the next. Blake followed, far more interested in her reaction to Van Gogh's masterpieces than the compositions themselves.

She was like one of the scenes the artist had painted, he mused. She'd come into his life shortly after Molly had, but he'd been so absorbed with the baby it had taken weeks for him to see her as something more than a quietly efficient nanny. The attraction had come slowly and built steadily, but the shock of learning that she'd deceived him—deceived them all—had altered the picture considerably. As had the annoying realization that he'd missed her as much as Molly had when she'd left Oklahoma City.

Yet every time he thought he had a handle on the woman, she added more layers, more bold brushstrokes to the composite. Her fierce loyalty to her cousin and refusal to betray Anne's trust irritated Blake to no end but he reluctantly, grudgingly respected her for it.

And Christ almighty! Yesterday's heat. That searing desire. He knew where his had sprung from. His hunger had been building since… Hell, he couldn't fix the exact point. He only knew that yesterday had stoked the need instead of satisfying it.

Now he'd found another layer to add to the mix—a woman in a black T-shirt and ball cap thoroughly enjoying the view of familiar images from a completely different perspective, just as Blake was viewing her. How many variations of her were there left to discover?

The question both intrigued and concerned him as he walked with her into the round-towered church that formed part of the original monastery. In keeping with the canons of poverty, chastity and obedience embraced by the Augustinian monks, the chapel was small and not overly ornate. The enclosed cloister beside it was also small, maybe thirty yards on each of its four sides. The cloister's outer walls were solid gray stone. Arched pillars framed the inner courtyard and formed a cool, shady colonnade. Sunlight angled through the intricately carved pillars to illuminate a stone sundial set amid a profusion of herbs and plants.

"Oooh," Grace murmured, her admiring gaze on the colonnade's intricately carved pillars. "I can almost see the monks walking two by two here, meditating or fingering their wooden rosaries. And Van Gogh aching to capture this juxtaposition of sunlight and shadow."

The artist couldn't have hurt any more than Blake did at the moment. The same intermingling of sun and shadow played across Grace's expressive face. The warm smile she tipped his way didn't help, either.

"I know you must have visited here several times during your stays in Saint-Rémy. Thanks for making another trek with me. I'm gaining a real appreciation for an artist I knew so little about before."

He masked his thoughts behind his customary calm. "You're welcome, but we're still at the beginning of the Van Gogh trail. You'll discover a good deal more about him as we go."

She made a sweeping gesture toward the far corner of the cloister. "Lead on, MacDuff."

They spent another half hour at Saint-Paul's. The windows in the two austere rooms where Van Gogh had lived and painted for more than a year gave narrow views of the gardens at the rear of the asylum and the rolling wheat fields beyond, both of which the artist had captured in numerous paintings. The garden's long rows of lavender had shed their purple blossoms, but the scent lingered in the air as Grace compared the scene with the plaques mounted along the garden's wall.

At the exit she lingered for a good five minutes in the spot reputedly depicted in *Starry Night,* arguably one of the artist's most celebrated canvases. The glowing golden balls flung across a dark cobalt sky utterly fascinated her and prompted Blake to purchase a framed print of the work at the gift shop. She started to protest that it was too expensive but bit back the words, knowing the stiff price wouldn't deter him any more than the price of the perfumed oil he'd purchased yesterday.

They stopped at the villa to drop off the purchase, then spent a leisurely two hours following the rest of the trail as it wound through the fields and narrow lanes Van Gogh painted when he was allowed to spend time away from the asylum. The trail ended in the center of town at the elegant eighteenth-century *hôtel* that had been converted to a museum and study center dedicated to the artist's life and unique style.

After another hour spent at the museum, Blake suggested lunch in town at a popular restaurant with more tables outside than in. Grace declared the location on one of Saint-Rémy's pedestrians-only streets perfect for people watching. Chin propped in both hands, she did just that while Blake scoped out the wine list. He went with a light, fruity local white and a melted ham-and-cheese sandwich, followed by a dessert of paper-thin crepes dribbling caramel sauce and powdered sugar. Grace opted for a crock of bouillabaisse brimming with carrots, peppers, tomatoes and celery in addition to five varieties of fresh fish, half-shelled oysters, shrimp and lobster. She passed on dessert after that feast, but couldn't resist sneaking a couple of bites of Blake's crepes.

They lingered at the restaurant, enjoying the wine and shade. Grace was sated and languid when they left, and distinctly sleepy-eyed when she settled into the sun-warmed leather of the convertible's passenger seat.

The crunch of tires on the villa's crushed-shell driveway woke her. She sat up, blinking, and laughed an apology.

"Sorry. I didn't mean to doze off on you."

"No problem." He braked to a halt just beyond the fountain of leaping, pawing horses. "At least you didn't go totally unconscious, like I did yesterday."

A hint of color rose in her cheeks. Blake sincerely hoped she was remembering the wild activity that had preceded yesterday's lengthy snooze. He certainly was. The color deepened when he asked with totally spurious nonchalance if she felt like a swim.

"I think I'll clean up a bit and see what's in the library. You go ahead if you want."

"I'll take a pass, too. I've got some emails I need to attend to."

"Okay. I'll, uh, see you later." She swung away, turned back. "Thanks again for sharing Van Gogh with me. I really enjoyed it."

"So did I."

This was what she'd wanted. What she'd insisted on. Grace muttered the mantra several times under her breath as she climbed the stairs to the second floor. Tugging off her ball cap, she freed her wind-tangled hair and tried a futile finger comb. When she opened the door to the Green Suite, she took two steps inside and stopped dead.

"Omigosh!"

Starry Night held a place of honor above the marble fireplace, all but obscuring the faint outline of whatever painting had hung there before. The print's cool, dark colors seemed to add depth to the silk wall coverings. The swirling stars and crescent moon blazed luminescent trails across the night sky, while the slumbering village below created a sense of quiet and peace. The dark, irregular, almost brooding shape dominating the left side of the print might seem a little sinister to some, but to Grace it was one of the cypress trees Van Gogh had captured in so many of his other works.

She walked into the suite, took a few steps to the side and marveled at how the stars seemed to follow her movements. Then she just stood for long moments, drinking in the print's vibrant colors and thinking of the man who'd obviously instructed it be hung where she could enjoy it during her stay.

Okay, no sense denying the truth when it was there, right in front of her eyes. Blake Dalton was pretty much everything she'd ever dreamed of in a husband. Smart, considerate, fun to be with, too handsome for words. And soooooo good with his hands and mouth and that hard, honed body of his.

She could fall in love with him so easily.

Already had, a little. All right, more than a little. She wouldn't let herself tumble all the way, though. Not with her cousin's memory hanging between them like a thin, dark curtain. As fragile as that curtain was, it formed an impenetrable barrier. Grace couldn't tell him the truth, and he couldn't trust her until she did.

Sighing, she turned away from the print and headed for the shower.

The curtain seemed even more impenetrable when she joined Blake for dinner that evening. As promised, Auguste had prepared his version of coquilles St. Jacques. It would be served, she'd been informed, in the small dining room. *Small* being a relative term, of course. Compared with the formal dining hall, which could seat thirty-six with elbow room to spare, this one was used for intimate dinners for ten or twelve. Silver candelabra anchored each end of the gleaming parquet-wood table. Between them sat a silver bowl containing a ginormous arrangement of white lilies and pink roses.

Blake had dressed for the occasion, Grace saw

when she entered the room. She felt a funny pang when she recognized the suit he'd worn at their wedding. He'd opted for no tie and left his white shirt open at the neck, though. That quieted her sudden jitters and let her appreciate his casual elegance.

He in turn appeared to approve of the sapphire-colored jersey sundress that had thankfully emerged from her suitcase wrinkle-free. Its slightly gathered skirt fell from a strapless, elasticized bodice. Earrings and a necklace of bright, chunky beads picked up the dress's color and added touches of purple and green, as well.

"Nice dress," Blake commented. "You look good in that shade of blue."

Hell, she looked good in any dress, any shade. Even better out of one. Manfully, he redirected his thoughts from the soft elastic gathers and refused to contemplate on how one small tug could bring them down.

"Would you care for a drink before dinner?" He nodded to the silver ice bucket on its stand. "There's champagne chilling."

"Who can say no to champagne?"

The wine was bottled exclusively for The Elms by the small vintner just outside Epernay Delilah had stumbled across a few years ago. She got such a kick out of presenting her friends and acquaintances with a gift of the private label that her sons had given up trying to convince her not everyone appreciated their champagne ultra brut.

With that in mind, he filled two crystal flutes, angled them to let the bubbles fizz and handed one to Grace.

"What shall we drink to?"

"How about starry nights, as depicted so beautifully by the print you had hung in my bedroom? Thank you for that."

"You're welcome." He chinked his flute to hers. "Here's to many, many starry nights."

He savored the wine's sharp, clean purity but wasn't surprised when Grace wrinkled her nose and regarded her glass with something less than a connoisseur's eye.

"It's, uh…"

"Very dry?"

"Very something."

"They make it with absolutely no sugar," Blake

explained, smiling. "It's the latest trend in champagne."

"If you say so."

"Try another sip. Mireille Guiliano highly recommends it in her book *French Women Don't Get Fat,*" he tacked on as additional inducement.

"Well, in that case…" She tipped her flute. The nose scrunch came a moment later. "Guess it takes some getting used to."

"Like our marriage," he agreed solemnly, then smiled as he relieved her of the drink. "We're learning to be nothing if not flexible, right? So I had another bottle put on ice just in case."

He made a serious dent in the ultra brut over dinner. Grace limited herself to one glass of the semi-sec but didn't debate or hesitate to accept a second serving of Auguste's decadent scallops au gratin. The chef himself presided over the serving tray and forked three shell-shaped ramekins onto her plate. Blake derived almost as much pleasure from her low, reverent groans of delight as he did from the succulent morsels and sinfully rich sauce.

The awkward moment came after dessert and

coffee. Blake could think of a number of ways to fill the rest of the evening. Unfortunately, he'd agreed to take wild, hot sex off the agenda. He had *not* agreed to table slow and sweet, but he gritted his teeth and decided to keep that as his ace in the hole.

"I think there are some playing cards in the library. Want to try your hand at gin rummy?"

"We could. Or…" Her eyes telegraphed a challenge. "We could check out the video room upstairs. I saw it had a Wii console. I'm pretty good at Ubongo, if I do say so myself."

"What's Ubongo?"

"Ahhhh." She crooked a finger, batted her lashes and laid on a heavy French accent. "*Come avec moi, monsieur,* and I will show you, yes?"

A month, even a week ago, Blake would never have imagined he'd spend the second night of his honeymoon frantically jabbing red buttons with his thumbs while jungle critters duked it out on a flat-screen TV and his bride snorted with derision at each miss…or that each snort would only make him want her more.

He fell asleep long after midnight still trying to decide how getting his butt kicked at Ubongo could put such a fierce lock on his heart. But he didn't realize just how fierce until the next afternoon.

Nine

When Grace came downstairs, Blake was pacing the sunny breakfast room with his phone to his ear. He speared a glance at her gauzy peasant skirt topped by a white lacy camisole, waggled his brows and gave a thumbs-up of approval.

She preened a little and returned the compliment. He'd gone casual this morning, too. Instead of his usual hand-tailored oxford shirt with the cuffs rolled up, he'd chosen a black, short-sleeved crew neck tucked into his tan slacks. The clingy fabric faithfully outlined the corded muscles of his shoulders and chest. Grace was enjoying the view when he finished one call and made a quick apology before taking the next.

"Sorry. We've just been notified of a possible nationwide transportation strike that could affect delivery from one of our subs here in France. I've got the plant manager on hold."

She flapped a hand. "Go ahead."

That discussion led to a third, this one a conference call with Alex and DI's VP for manufacturing. Although it was still the middle of the night back in the States, both men were evidently working the problem hard. Grace caught snatches of their discussion while she scarfed down another of Auguste's incredible breakfasts.

Blake apologized again when he finished the call. "Looks like I'll have to hang close to the villa this morning while we refine our contingency plan. Alex said to tell you he's sorry for butting into your honeymoon."

Her honeymoon, she noted. Not his.

"No problem," she replied, shrugging off the little sting. "I want to do some shopping. I'll walk into town this morning."

When she left the villa an hour later, she saw

vehicles jammed into every available parking space along the tree-shaded road leading into the heart of town. They were her first clue something was happening. The bright red umbrellas and canvas-topped booths that now sprouted like mushrooms in every nook and cranny of the town provided the second.

Delighted, Grace discovered it was market day in Saint-Rémy. Busy sellers offered everything from books and antiques to fresh vegetables, strings of sausages and giant wheels of cheese. A good many of the stalls displayed the products in the dreamy colors of Provence—pale yellows and pinks and lavenders of the soaps, earthy reds and golds in the pottery and linens.

She wandered the crowded streets and lanes, sniffing the heady scents, eagerly accepting free samples when offered. She bought boxed soaps for friends back in San Antonio, a hand-sewn sundress and floppy-brimmed hat exploding with sunflowers for Molly, a small but exquisitely worked antique cameo brooch as a peace offering for Delilah.

She'd thanked the dealer and was turning away

when a wooden case at the back of the umbrella-shaded stall caught her eye. It held what looked like antique man stuff—intricately worked silver shoe buckles, pearl stickpins, a gold-rimmed monocle with a black ribbon loop.

And one ring.

Compared with the other ornate pieces in the case, the ring was relatively plain. The only design on the wide yellow gold band was a fleur-de-lis set in onyx. At least, Grace assumed those glittering black stones were onyx. She learned her mistake when the dealer lifted the ring from the case to give her a closer look.

"Madame has a good eye," he commented. "This piece is very old and very rare. From the seventeenth century. Those are black sapphires in the center."

"I didn't know there *were* black sapphires."

"But yes! Hold the ring to the light. You will see the fineness of their cut."

She did as instructed and couldn't tell squat about the cut, but the stones threw back a black fire that made Grace gasp and gave the dealer the scent of a deal in the making. He added subtle pressure by dropping some of the ring's history.

"It is rumored to have once belonged to the Count of Provence. But the last of the count's descendants lost his head in the Revolution and the rabble sacked and burned his *hôtel,* so we have no written records of this ring. No—how do you call it? Certificate of authenticity. Only this rumor, you understand."

Grace didn't care. She'd walked out of Judge Honeywell's office wearing a band of diamonds. Blake's ring finger was still bare. She didn't need a certificate to rectify the situation. Those shimmering black sparks were authentic enough for her.

"How much is it?"

He named a figure that made her gulp until she realized it was a starting point for further negotiations. She countered. He shook his head and came back with another price. She sighed and put the ring back in the case. He plucked it out again.

"But look at these stones, madame. This workmanship."

"I don't know if it will fit my husband," she argued.

"It can always be resized."

He dropped his glance to the sparkling gems circling her finger. His expression said she could certainly afford to have it fitted, but he cut the price by another fifty euros. Grace did the conversion to dollars in her head, gulped again and tried to remember the exact balance in her much-depleted bank account.

She could cover it. Barely. Squaring her shoulders, she took the plunge. "Do you take Visa?"

The velvet bag containing the ring remained tucked in her purse when she returned to the villa. A local official had delivered documents couriered in from some government source, and Blake had invited her to join them for lunch. The woman was lively company and was delighted to learn Blake intended to show his bride Saint-Rémy's ancient Roman ruins. She also warned they must go that very afternoon, as the archeological site could be affected if the transportation unions went on strike the following day as they'd threatened.

Grace couldn't see the connection but didn't argue when Blake said he was satisfied with his review of the contingency plans and was free to roam for a few hours. Before they left the villa, though, he made sure his mobile phone was fully charged, then tucked it close at hand in the breast pocket of his shirt.

The monuments she'd spotted through the trees yesterday were even more impressive up close and personal. Blake parked in a dusty, unpaved lot filled with cars and what turned out to be school buses. Grace had to smile at the noisy, exuberant teens piling out of the buses.

"I've taken my classes on a few field trips like this one," she commented. "It's always tough to judge how much of what they'll see actually sinks in."

Not much, Blake guessed. At least for the young, would-be studs in the crowd. As both he and his brother could verify, the attention of boys that age centered a whole lot more on girls in tight jeans than ancient ruins.

Boys of any age, actually. Grace wasn't in jeans, but she snagged more than one admiring look from the male students and their teachers as she and Blake joined the line straggling along the dirt path to *Les Antiques.*

The two monuments gleamed white in the afternoon sun. Blake couldn't remember which triumph the massive arch was supposed to commemorate—the conquest of Marseille, he thought—but he knew the perfectly preserved marble tower beside the arch had served as a mausoleum for a prominent Roman family. Luckily, descriptive plaques alongside each monument provided the details in both French and English.

Blake wasn't surprised that the teacher in Grace had to read every word, much as she had on the Van Gogh trail yesterday. Peering over the heads of the kids, she glanced from the plaque to the intricate pattern decorating the underside of the arch.

"This is interesting. Those flowers and vines represent the fertility of 'the Roman Province,' aka *Provence.* I didn't know that's where the region's name came from."

Two of the teens obviously thought she'd addressed the comment to them. One turned and pulled an earbud from his ear. The other tucked what looked like a sketchbook under his arm and asked politely, *"Pardon, madame?"*

"The name, Provence." She gestured to the sign. "It's from the Latin."

"Ah, oui."

Blake hid a smile as the boys looked her over with the instinctive appreciation of the male of the species. They obviously liked what they saw. And who wouldn't? Her hair was a wind-tossed tangle of pale silk, and the skin displayed all too enticingly by the white lace camisole had been warmed to a golden tan by the hot Provencal sun. Not surprisingly, the boys lagged behind while the rest of their group posed and snapped pictures of each other under the watchful eyes of their teachers.

"You are from the U.S.?" the taller of the two asked.

"I am," she confirmed. "From Texas."

"Ahhh, Texas. Cowboys, yes? And cows with the horns like this."

When he extended his arms, Grace grinned and spread hers as far as they would go. "More like this."

"*Oui?*"

"*Oui.* And you? Where are you from?"

"Lyon, madame."

The shorter kid was as eager as his pal to show off his English. "We study the Romans," he informed Grace, his earbud dangling. "They were in Lyon, as in many other parts of Provence. You have seen the coliseum in Arles and the Pont du Gard?"

"Not yet."

"But you must!" The taller kid whipped his sketchbook from under his arm, flipped up the lid and riffled through the pages. "Here is the Pont du Gard."

Grace was impressed. So was Blake. He'd visited the famous aqueduct a number of times. The kid's drawings captured both the incredible engineering and soaring beauty of its three tiers of arches.

One of the teachers came over at that point to see what his students were up to. When he discovered Grace was a teacher, he joined the kids in describing the Roman sites she should be sure to visit while in the south of France. He also provided her a list of the architectural and historical items of interest he'd tasked his students to search out at *Les Antiques* and the adjoining town of Glanum.

"What a good idea," Grace exclaimed as she skimmed the Xeroxed four pages. "It's like a treasure hunt."

"The class searches in teams," the teacher explained. "You should join us. You will gain a far better appreciation of this site."

"I'd love to but…" She threw Blake a questioning glance. "Do we have time?"

"Sure."

"We can team up."

Blake gauged the boys' reaction to that with a single glance. "You and these fellows do the hunting," he said easily. "I'll follow along."

List in hand, she joined the search. Her unfeigned interest and ready smile made willing slaves of her two teammates. Preening like young gamecocks, they translated the background history of the first item on the list, and crowed with delight when they collectively spotted the chained captives at the base of the arch representing Rome's might.

Blake found a shady spot and rested his hips against a fallen marble block, watching as Grace and her team searched out two additional items on the arch and three on the tall, pillared tower of the mausoleum. He wondered if the boys had any idea that she let them do the discovering. Or that her seemingly innocent questions about the translations forced them to delve much deeper into the history of the site than they otherwise would have. Those two, at least, were going home experts on *Les Antiques*.

The hunt took them across the street and down another hundred yards to the entrance to Glanum. Unlike the arch and mausoleum, access to the town itself was controlled and active excavations were under way at several spots along its broad main street. Despite the roped-off areas, there was still plenty to explore. The students poked into the thermal furnaces that heated the baths, clambered over the uneven stones of a Hellenistic temple and followed the narrow, twisty track through the ravine at the far end of town to the spring that had convinced Gauls to settle this site long before the Romans arrived.

Grace was right there with her team, carefully picking her way down a flight of broken marble steps to the pool fed by the sacred spring. The fact that she could translate the Latin inscription dedicating the pool to Valetudo, the Roman goddess of health, scored her considerable brownie points with the kids. The delight they took in her company scored even more with Blake.

He could guess the kind of dreams those boys would have tonight. He'd had the same kind at their age. Still had 'em, he admitted wryly, his gaze locked on his wife.

The hunt finished, Grace exchanged email addresses with her teammates and their teacher before walking back to the car with Blake.

"You were really good with those kids," he commented.

"Thanks. I enjoy interacting with teens. Most of them have such lively minds, although the mood swings and raging hormones can be a pain at times."

Their footsteps stirred the dust on the unpaved path. A car whizzed by on the road to the mountain village high up in the Alpilles. The scents of summer lingered on the still air. Blake grasped her elbow to guide her around a rough patch, then slid his hand down to take hers.

He saw her glance down at the fingers interlacing hers. A small line creased her forehead, but she didn't ease her hand away until they reached the convertible. Blake chalked the frown up to the unsettled nature of their marriage and started to open the passenger door for her. She planted her hip against the door, stopping him.

"I bought you something while I was in town this morning." She fished a small velvet bag out of her purse. "It's not much. But I saw it and thought of you and our time here in France and… Well, I just wanted you to have it."

When he untied the strings, a heavy gold ring rolled into his palm. The fleur-de-lis embedded in its center flashed a rainbow of sparks.

"The dealer said it's an antique. He thinks it

once belonged to the Count of Provence, but there's no documentation to support that claim." She looked from the ring to him with a mix of uncertainty and shyness. "Do you like it?"

"Very much. Thank you."

The heartfelt thanks dissolved both the shyness and uncertainty. "You're welcome."

The inquiries Blake had run into her finances told him she must have maxed out her credit card to buy the ring, but he knew better than to ruin the moment by asking if she needed a quick infusion of funds. He showed his appreciation instead by tilting the design up to the light.

"The stones are brilliantly cut."

"That's what the dealer said."

"He said right. You rarely find sapphires with so many facets."

"How'd you guess they're sapphires?"

Grinning, he lowered the ring. "Mother has me take care of insurance appraisals and certificates of authenticity for all her jewelry. She's got more rare stones in her collection than the Smithsonian."

"I don't doubt it. Here," she said when he started to slide it on. "Let me."

She eased the ring onto his finger, then hesitated with the band just above the knuckle.

"With this ring…"

The soft words hit with a jolt, ricocheting around in Blake's chest as she worked the ring over his knuckle. It was a tight fit, but the gold band finally slid on.

"…I thee wed."

Grace finished in a whisper and folded her hand over his. Blake didn't respond. He couldn't. His throat was as tight as a drum.

"I can recall every minute in Judge Honeywell's office," she confessed on a shaky laugh. "I can hear the words, replay the entire scene in vivid Technicolor. Yet…"

She glanced around the dusty parking lot, brought her gaze back to his.

"This is the first time I feel as though it's all for real."

"It is real. More than I imagined it could be back there in the judge's office."

His hand tightened, crushing hers against the

heavy gold band. She glanced down, startled, then met his gaze again.

"Let me take you home and show you just how real it's become for me."

Blake had no doubts. None at all. He made the short drive to the villa on a surge of adrenaline and desire so thick and heavy it clamped his fists on the steering wheel.

Uncertainty didn't hit until he followed Grace up the stairs and into the cool confines of the Green Suite. When she turned to face him, he half expected her to retreat again, insist they go back to cool and polite.

He'd never wanted a woman the way he wanted this one. Never loved one the way he did his bright, engaging, sun-kissed bride. The fierce acknowledgment rattled him almost as much as the hunger gnawing at his insides. He could slam on the brakes if he had to, though. It would damned near kill him, but he could do it. All she had to do was…

"Lock the door."

It took a second or two for his brain to process

the soft command. Another couple for him to click the old-fashioned latch into place. When he turned back, she reached for the top button on her camisole.

His uncharacteristic doubts went up in a blaze of heat. With a low growl, he brushed her hands aside. "I've been fantasizing about popping these buttons since you came downstairs this morning."

He forced himself to undo them slowly. He wanted the pleasure of baring the slopes of her breasts inch by tantalizing inch. But his greedy pleasure splintered into something close to pain when he peeled back the cottony fabric and revealed the half bra underneath. With a concentration that popped sweat on his brow, he slid the camisole off her shoulders.

Damn! He was as jerky and eager as any of the adolescents they'd encountered this afternoon. Grace was the steady one. She displayed no hint of embarrassment or shyness when the camisole slithered down her arms and dropped to the carpet.

She reached back and unhooked her bra. The

movement was so essentially female, so erotic and arousing. Blake ached for the feel of her smooth, firm flesh against his. But when he dragged his shirt free of his slacks, she copied his earlier move and brushed his hands aside.

"My turn."

Just as he had, she took her time. Her palms edged under the shirt, flattened on his stomach, glided upward. Blake bent so she could get it off over his head. His breath razored in, then out when her hands slid south again. A smile played in her eyes when she found his belt buckle.

"I've been fantasizing about *this* since I came downstairs this morning."

"Okay, that's it!"

He had her in his arms in one swoop and marched to the bed.

Ten

The session in the swimming pool had sprung the beast in Blake. This time, he was damned if he would let it slip its leash. He kept every move slow and deliberate as he dragged the brocade coverlet back and stretched Grace out on the soft, satiny sheets.

He took his time removing the rest of her clothes, and his. As he joined her on the cool, satiny sheets, his eyes feasted on her lithe curves. Tan lines made a noticeable demarcation at her shoulders and upper thighs. The skin between was soft and pale and his to explore.

"Too bad Van Gogh isn't around to paint you."

He stroked the creamy slopes and valleys. "You would have inspired him to even greater genius."

"I seriously doubt that."

"Well, you certainly inspire me. Like here…"

He brushed a kiss across her mouth.

"And here…"

His lips traced her cheeks and feathered her lids.

"And here…"

Mounding her breast, he teased the nipple with his teeth and tongue until it puckered stiff and tight. Blake gave the other breast equal attention and got a hint of the anguish Van Gogh must have suffered over his masterpieces. He was feeling more than a little tormented himself as he explored the landscape of his wife's body.

She didn't lay passive during the investigation. She flung one arm above her head, brought it down again to plane her hand over his shoulder and down his back. Fingers eager, she kneaded his hip and butt.

Blake felt the muscles low in his belly jerk in response but refused to rush the pace. His palm slid over her rib cage, down her belly. Her stomach hollowed under his touch, and a knee came up as he threaded the dark gold hair of her mound. He slid one finger inside the hot, slick lips, then two, and pressed the tight bud between with his thumb.

Her breath was a fast, shallow rasp now. His was almost as harsh. And when she rolled and nudged him onto his back, it shot damned near off the chart.

She went up on an elbow and conducted her own exploration. Just as slowly. Just as thoroughly. His chin and throat got soft kisses, his shoulder a nuzzle and a teasing nip. She followed by lightly scraping a fingertip down his chest and through hair that arrowed toward his groin.

"Now here," she said with a wicked grin as her fingers closed around him, "we have a real masterpiece."

"You won't hear me argue with that," he returned, his grin matching hers.

She gave a huff of laughter and stroked him, gently at first, then with increasing pressure. The friction coiled him as tight as a centrifuge, but he was confident in his ability to extend this period of mutual discovery awhile longer yet. Right up until she bent down, took him in her mouth and shot his confidence all to hell and back.

His breath left on a hiss. Everything below his waist went on red alert. He managed to hang on for a few moments longer but knew his control was about to blow.

"Grace…"

The low warning brought her head up. Her lips were wet and glistening, her eyes cloudy with desire. When he would have reversed positions, she preempted him by hooking a leg over his thighs. She guided him into her, gasping when he thrust upward, and dropped forward to plant her hands on his chest. The skin over her cheeks was stretched tight. Her hair formed a tangled curtain. Blake had never seen anything more beautiful or seductive in his life.

"Forget Van Gogh," he said gruffly. "Not even he could do you justice."

He shoved his hands through her hair and brought her down for a kiss that was as fierce as it was possessive.

* * *

Grace came awake with a twitch. Something rasped like fine sandpaper against her temple. Blake's chin, she decided after a hazy moment. Unshaven and bristly. Deciding to ignore the movement, she burrowed her nose deeper into the warm crevice between his neck and shoulder.

"Grace?"

"Mmmm."

"You awake?"

"Nuh-uh."

"No?"

He shifted, and the chin made another scrape. Grace raised her head and squinted at the dim shadows wreathing the room.

"Whatimeizzit?"

"Close to six, I think."

"Jeez!"

Her head dropped. Her cheek thumped his chest. She tried to drift back into sleep but laughter rumbled annoyingly under her ear.

"Not a morning person, I take it."

"Not a 6:00 a.m. person," she mumbled, sounding sulky even to herself.

"I'll keep that in mind for future reference."

It took a few moments for that to penetrate her sleepy fog. When it did, she pushed up on an elbow and shoved her hair out of her eyes. She wasn't awake enough to address the subject of the future head-on. Or maybe she just didn't have the nerve. Still a little grumpy, she went at it sideways.

"Are you? A morning person, I mean?"

"Pretty much." An apologetic smile creased his whiskery cheeks. "I've been awake for an hour or so."

She groaned and would have made a dive for the pillows, but he shifted again. She ended up lying on her side, facing him, with her head propped on a hand and her thoughts hijacked by a worry about morning breath. She ran a quick tongue over her teeth. They didn't feel too fuzzy. And her lips weren't caked with drool, thank God! She refused to think about her uncombed hair and unwashed face. Or how much she needed to pee.

Blake, of course, looked totally gorgeous in the dim light. A lazy smile lit his wide-awake blue eyes, and he was tantalizingly naked above the rumpled sheets. He even smelled good. Sort of musky and masculine and warm.

When she finished inspecting the little swirl of dark gold hair around his navel and brought her gaze back to his face, she saw his smile had taken on a different slant. Less lazy. More serious.

"I did some thinking while I was lying here waiting for you to rejoin the living."

She guessed from his expression what he'd been cogitating over but asked anyway. "About?"

"Us."

The arm propping her up suddenly felt shaky. Did he want to alter their still-evolving relationship? Renegotiate the contract? After last night, she was certainly open to different terms and conditions. Still, she had to work to keep her voice steady.

"And what did you conclude, counselor?"

"I want to make this work, Grace. You, me, our marriage."

"I thought we were making it work."

"Bad word choice. I meant make it real."

He reached over to tuck a tangled strand behind

her ear. She held her breath until he'd positioned it to his satisfaction.

"I want to spend the rest of my life with you. You and Molly and the children we might have together."

Oh, God! Were they really having this discussion with her teeth unbrushed and her face crumpled into sleep lines? She couldn't fall on his chest again, lock her mouth on his and show him how much she wanted the exact same things.

"Hold on."

Surprise blanked his face at the terse order. A swift frown followed almost instantly as she threw off the sheet.

"I'll be right back."

She spent all of three minutes in the bathroom. When she emerged, he was sitting with his back against the padded silk headboard. The scowl remained, but the fact that she was still naked seemed to reassure him. That, and the joy she didn't try to disguise when she scrambled onto the bed and knelt facing him.

"Okay, I can respond properly now. Repeat what you said, word for word."

He hooked a brow and repeated obediently, "I want to spend the rest of my life with you."

"Me and..." she prompted.

"You and Molly and the children we might have together."

A giddy happiness gathered in her throat, but she had to make sure. "And you can live with the fact that I won't...can't tell you Anne's secrets?"

"I don't like it," he admitted honestly, "but I can live with it."

"Then I say we go for it. Molly, more babies, the whole deal."

The laughter came back, and with it a tenderness that made her heart hurt.

"Whew! You had me worried there for a moment."

"Yes, well, for future reference, you probably want to wait until I've brushed my teeth to spring something like that on me."

"I'll add that to the list," he said as she framed his face with both hands.

She reveled in the scrape of his whiskery cheeks, amazed and humbled at the prospect of sharing the months and years ahead with this

smart, handsome, incredible man. Every tumultuous hope for their future filled her heart as she
leaned in and sealed their new contract.

Given the rocky start to her marriage, Grace
would never have believed her honeymoon would
turn into the stuff that dreams are made of.

Last-minute negotiations averted the threatened
strike, so no further business issues intruded and
Grace had her husband's undivided attention. As
she'd already discovered, he woke early and dis-
gustingly energized. She wasn't exactly a sloth,
but she did prefer to open her eyes to sunshine
versus a dark, shadowy dawn. They compro-
mised by making love late into the night, every
night, and in the morning only after she'd come
fully alert. Afternoons and early evenings were
up for grabs.

They also spent long hours learning about the
person they'd married. Grace already knew Blake
liked to read but until now had only seen him
buried behind *The Wall Street Journal* or *The
New York Times* or the latest nonfiction bestseller. She raided the library on one of Provence's

rare rainy afternoons and wooed him away from the real world by curling up with a copy of one of her all-time favorites. He didn't exactly go into raptures over *Jane Eyre* but agreed the heroine did develop some backbone toward the end of the story.

Grace returned the favor by digging into the bestseller he'd picked up at a store in town that stocked books in English as well as French. Although she had a good grasp of American history, she never expected to lose herself in a biography of James Garfield. But historian Candace Millard packed high drama and nail-biting suspense into her riveting *Destiny of the Republic: A Tale of Madness, Medicine and the Murder of a President.*

Aside from that one rainy afternoon, they spent most of the daylight hours outside in the pool or in town or exploring Provence. The Roman ruins of Glanum had fired Grace's interest in the area's other sights. The coliseum at Arles and arch of ramparts in Orange more than lived up to her expectations. The undisputed highlight of their journey into the far-distant past, however, was the gastronomical masterpiece of a picnic Auguste had prepared for their jaunt to the three-tiered Pont du Gard aqueduct. They consumed truffle-stuffed breast of capon and julienne carrots with baby pearl onions in great style on the pebbly banks of the river meandering under the ancient aqueduct.

They jumped more than a dozen centuries when they toured the popes' palace at Avignon. Constructed when a feud between Rome and the French King Philip IV resulted in two competing papacies, the palace was a sprawling city of stone battlements and turrets that dominated a rocky outcropping overlooking the Rhône. From there the natural next step was a visit to Châteauneuf du Pape, another palace erected by the wine-loving French popes to promote the area's viticulture. It was set on a hilltop surrounded by vineyards and olive groves and offered a private, prearranged tasting of rich red blends made from grenache, counoise, Syrah and muscadine grapes.

Each day brought a new experience. And each day Grace fell a little more in love with her husband. The nights only added to the intensity of

her feelings. The unabashed romantic in her
wanted to spin out indefinitely this time when
she had Blake all to herself. Her more practi-
cal self kept interrupting that idyllic daydream
with questions. Like where they would live. And
whether she would transfer her teaching certificate from Texas to Oklahoma. And how Delilah
would react to the altered relationship between
her son and Grace.

Her two sides came into direct conflict the
bright, sunny morning they drove to the open-air
market in a small town some twenty miles away.
L'Isle sur la Sorgue's market was much larger
than Saint-Rémy's and jam-packed with tourists in addition to serious shoppers laying in the
day's provisions, but the exuberant atmosphere
and lovely old town bisected by the Sorgue River
made browsing the colorful stalls a delight.

For a late breakfast they shared a cup of cappuccino and a waffle cone of succulent straw-
berries capped with real whipped cream. They
followed that with samples of countless varieties
of cheese and sausage and fresh-baked pastries.
So many that when Blake suggested lunch at one

of the little bistros lining the town's main street, Grace shook her head and held up the paper bag containing the wrapped leek-and-goat-cheese tarts they'd just purchased.

"One of these is enough for me. All I need is something to wash it down with."

He pointed her to the benches set amid the weeping willows gracing the riverbank. The trees' leafy ribbons trailed in the gently flowing water and threw a welcome blanket of shade over the grassy bank.

"Sit tight," Blake instructed. "We passed a fresh-fruit stand a few stalls back. They mix up smoothies like you wouldn't believe. Any flavor favorites?"

"I'm good for anything except kiwi. I can't stand the hairy little things."

"No kiwi in yours. Got it. One more item to add to our future reference list."

The list was getting longer, Grace thought with a smile as she sat on the grass and stretched out her legs. Other people were scattered along the bank. Mothers and fathers and grandparents lounged at ease, with each generation keeping a vigilant eye on the youngsters tempting fate at the river's edge. A little farther away one young couple had gone horizontal, so caught up in the throes of youthful passion that they appeared in imminent danger of locking nose rings. Their moves started slow but soon gathered enough steam to earn a gentle rebuke from two nuns walking by on the sidewalk above and a not-so-gentle admonition from a father entertaining two lively daughters while his wife nursed a third. His words were low and in French, but Grace caught the drift. So did the lovers. Shrugging, they rolled onto their stomachs and confined their erotic exchange to whispers and Eskimo nose rubs.

Grace's glance drifted from them to the mother nursing her child. As serene as a Madonna in a painting by a grand master, she held the baby in the crook of her elbow and gently eased the nipple between the gummy lips. She didn't bother with a drape or cover over her shoulder, but performed the most natural task in the world oblivious to passersby. Men quickly averted their eyes. Some women smiled, some looked as though they were recounting memories of performing this same act, and one or two showed an expression of envy.

The scene stirred a welter of emotions in Grace she'd thought long buried. She'd prayed during Anne's troubled marriage that her cousin wouldn't get pregnant and produce a child to tie her even more to Jack Petrie. So what did Anne do after escaping the nightmare of her marriage and slowly, agonizingly regaining her self-respect? She fell for a high-powered attorney, turned up pregnant, panicked and ran again. Only this time she didn't run far or fast enough to escape her fear. Anne landed in a hospital in San Diego, and her baby landed in Grace's arms.

Grace had done her damndest not to let Molly wrap her soft, chubby arms wrap around her heart. It had been a losing battle right from the start. Almost the first moment she held Anne's daughter in her arms, she'd started working a contingency plan in her mind. She would keep Molly under wraps while she let it leak to friends that she was pregnant. Once she was sure word had gotten back to Anne's sadistic husband, she would take a leave of absence from her job and play out a fake pregnancy somewhere where no one knew her. Then she'd raise Molly as her own.

Instead, her dying cousin had begged Grace to deliver the baby to her father. Grace had conceded. Reluctantly. She understood the rationale, accepted that the child belonged with her father. The weeks Grace had spent with the Daltons as Molly's temporary nanny had only reinforced that inescapable fact. But the bond between her and Molly had become a chain around her heart. She'd dreaded with every ounce of her soul breaking that chain and walking away from both the child and the dynamic, charismatic Daltons. Now the chain remained intact.

Drawing up her legs, Grace rested her chin on her knees. She still needed to put a contingency plan into operation. She couldn't take the chance that Anne's sadistic husband might discover Grace had married a man with a young baby. Petrie would check Blake out, discover he wasn't a widower, wonder how he'd acquired an infant daughter just about the same time Grace came into his life.

She would contact a few of her friends in San Antonio, she decided grimly. Imply she'd met someone late last year, maybe during the Christmas break, and had spent the spring semester and summer vacation adjusting to the unexpected result. Then Blake Dalton had swooped in and convinced her to marry him.

Those deliberately vague seeds would sprout and spread to other coworkers. Eventually some version of the story might reach Jack Petrie. It should be enough to throw him off Molly's scent. It had to be!

Lost in her contingency planning, she didn't hear Blake's return until he came up beside her.

"One strawberry-peach-mango combo for you. One blueberry-banana for me."

She moved the sack with the tarts to make room for him on the patch of grass. Legs folded, he sank down with a loose-limbed athletic grace and passed her a plastic cup heaped with whipped cream and a dark red cherry. They ate in companionable silence, enjoying the scene.

The Sorgue River flowed smooth and green just yards away. The young lovers were still stretched out nose-to-nose. The father was hunkered down at the river's bank within arm's reach of his two laughing, wading daughters. His wife held the baby against her shoulder now and was patting up a burp.

Grace let a spoonful of her smoothie slide down a throat that suddenly felt raw and tight. This baby looked nothing like Molly. Her eyes were nowhere near as bright a blue, and instead of Mol's golden curls, she had feathery, flyaway black hair her mother had obviously tried to tame with a jaunty pink bow. Yet when she waved tiny, dimpled fists and gummed a smile, Grace laughed and returned it.

Blake caught the sound and followed her line of sight. Hooking an elbow on his knee, he watched the baby's antics until she let loose with a burp that carried clearly across the grass. After another, quieter encore, her mother slid her down into nursing position.

When Grace gave a small sigh, Blake studied her profile. He wasn't surprised by what he saw there, or by the plea in her eyes when she turned to him.

"I've had an incredible time in Provence," she said slowly. "Every day, every night with you has been a fantasy come true."

She threw another look at the baby, and he read her thoughts.

"I miss Molly, too," he admitted with a wry grin. "Let's go home."

Eleven

His mind made up, Blake moved with characteristic speed and decisiveness. While he and Grace threaded through the crowded market to their car, he used his cell phone to run a quick check of flight schedules for Dalton International's air fleet. The corporate jet was on the wrong side of the Atlantic, so he booked first-class seats on a commercial nonstop flight to Dallas leaving late that afternoon. With the time differential and the short hop to Oklahoma, they would get home at almost the same hour they departed France.

That left Grace barely an hour to throw her things together and say goodbye to Auguste and the rest of the staff. Blake's farewells included exorbitant gratuities for each member of the staff and a promise to bring madame back for a longer stay very soon.

The rush of leaving and her eagerness to get back to Molly carried Grace halfway across the Atlantic. Having Blake beside her in the luxurious first-class cabin staved off fatigue during the remainder of the trip. His low-voiced, less than complimentary commentary on the action flick they watched together had her giggling helplessly and the other passengers craning to see what was on their screens.

Fatigue didn't factor in until after the plane change in Dallas. Fatigue, and a serious case of nerves about coming face-to-face with Blake's mother again. Delilah had let loose with both barrels at her last meeting with Grace. The note from her that Alex delivered in San Antonio had much the same tone. She hadn't been happy about the hurry-up wedding and warned that she'd have something to say about it when the newlyweds returned from France.

Grace couldn't imagine how the redoubtable

Dalton matriarch would react to the altered relationship between her son and his bride. Delilah must have known Blake proposed for strictly utilitarian reasons. Mostly utilitarian, anyway. Would she believe his feelings could undergo a major shift in such a short time? Probably not. Grace could hardly believe it herself.

By the time they turned onto the sweeping drive that led to Delilah's Nichols Hills mansion, dread curled like witches' fingers in her stomach. Then the front door flew open and she saw at a glance she'd underestimated Delilah. The older woman took one look at them and gave a whoop that boomed like a cannon shot in the brisk September air.

"I knew it!" she announced gleefully as they mounted the front steps. "No one can resist the fatal combination of Provence and Auguste. Especially two people who were so danged hot for each other."

"Don't you ever get tired of being right?" Blake drawled as he bent to kiss her cheek.

"Never." Blue eyes only a shade lighter than

her son's skewered Grace. "And that's something for you to remember, too, missy. Now get over here and so I can give my newest daughter-in-law a hug."

Enfolded in a bone-crunching embrace and a cloud of outrageously expensive perfume, Grace made the instant transition from employee and former nanny to member of the family. She was so grateful to this fierce and occasionally over-bearing woman that she found herself battling tears.

"Thank you for trusting me with Molly and for...and for...everything."

"We should be thanking you." The hug got tighter, Delilah's voice gruffer. "You brought Molly to us in the first place."

Both women were sniffling when they separated. Embarrassed by her uncharacteristic descent into sentimentality, Delilah flapped a hand toward the stairs.

"I expect you want to see the baby. She's up in the nursery. I just heard her on the monitor, waking up from her nap."

The last time Grace had climbed this magnificent circular staircase was as an employee in Delilah's home. She couldn't quite get a grip on her feelings as she ascended them alongside Blake, anxious to embrace the baby now making come-get-me noises from the room on the left at the top of the stairs. Nerves played a major role. Excitement and eagerness bubbled in there, too. But mostly it was sheer incredulity that she now had the right to claim this man and this child as hers.

When they swept into the nursery Delilah had furnished so swiftly and so lavishly, Molly was standing up in the crib. Her downy blond hair formed a spiky halo and her blue eyes tracked their entrance with a touch of impatience, as if asking what took them so long.

Grace's heart melted into a puddle of mush at the sight of her. It disintegrated even more when Molly gave a gurgle of delight and raised her arms.

"Gace!"

Half laughing, half sobbing, Grace swept the baby out of the crib.

* * *

September rolled out and October came in with a nighttime temperature dip into the forties and fifties. As the weeks flew by, a nasty little corner of Grace's mind kept insisting this couldn't last. Sometime, somehow, she would pay for the joy she woke up with every morning. But her busy, busy days and nights spent in Blake's arms buried that niggling thought under an avalanche of others.

Their first order of business was finding a house. Rather than move Molly's nursery to Blake's bachelor pad during the hectic process of inspecting available properties, they accepted Delilah's invitation to occupy the guest wing of her mansion. So naturally both Molly and Delilah went with Grace to check out the possibilities when Blake got tied up at work. Julie, too, when she wasn't flying or distracted by the business of setting up the home she and Alex had recently moved into.

Grace worried at first that Delilah might try to push her toward something big and splashy, but her mother-in-law was motivated by only one goal. She wanted her granddaughter close enough to spoil at will. So she was thrilled when Grace settled on a recently renovated half-timbered home less than a mile from the Dalton mansion. The two-story house sat well back from the street on a one-acre lot shaded by tall pines. Grace had fallen in love with its oak floors and open, sunny kitchen at first sight, but balked at the five bedrooms until Blake convinced her they could convert one to an entertainment center and one to an exercise room unless and until they needed it for other purposes.

Once the house was theirs, Grace faced the daunting prospect of filling its empty rooms. She thought about tackling one room at a time, but Delilah graciously offered the services of her decorator to coordinate the overall scheme.

"Take her up on it," Julie urged during a weekend brunch at their mother-in-law's.

The two brides lolled on the sunlit terrace, keeping a lazy eye on Molly in her net playpen while their husbands checked football scores in the den. Delilah had taken her other guest to the library to show him some faded photographs she'd unearthed from her early days working the oil fields with her husband. Grace found it extremely interesting that Julie's irascible partner, Dusty Jones, had apparently become a regular visitor to the Nichols Hills mansion.

"The decorator is good," her new sister-in-law asserted. "Really good."

Grace could hardly disagree. She'd lived in these opulent surroundings for several months as Molly's nanny. The Lalique chandeliers and magnificent antiques suited Delilah's flair and flamboyance, but Grace had lived in constant dread of Molly spitting up all over one of the hand-woven Italian silk seat cushions.

"Trust me," Julie urged. "Victor will help you achieve just the look you want. He understood right away that I wanted to go clean and uncluttered in our place. I've agreed with almost everything he's suggested so far."

"Surprising everyone concerned," Grace drawled, "yourself included."

"True," the redhead agreed, laughing. "I do tend to formulate strong opinions about things... as Alex frequently points out."

Marriage agreed with her, Grace thought. She looked so relaxed and happy with her auburn hair spilling over her shoulders and her fingers playing with the gold pendant Alex had given her as an engagement gift. The figure depicted on the intricately carved disk was the Inca god who supposedly rose from Lake Titicaca in the time of darkness to create the sun, the moon and the stars. Julie, who'd spent several years ferrying cargo in and out of remote airstrips in South America, had told Grace the god's name but she could never remember it.

"Might as well bow to the inevitable and give Victor a call," Julie advised, stretching languidly. "If you don't, Delilah will just invite him for cocktails one evening and make the poor guy go over your house plans room by room while she pours martinis down his throat."

"Okay, okay. I'll call him."

The two women sat in companionable silence. They'd known each other for only a few months but had become friends in that short time. Marrying twins had solidified the bond. It had also given them unique perspectives into each other's lives.

Grace had worried that her being the one to provide indisputable proof that Blake was Molly's father might drive a wedge between the brothers. Or between her and Alex. Until those final DNA results had come back, the preponderance of evidence had pointed to Alex as the most likely father. He'd taken the baby into his heart and had rearranged his life around her. The home he and Julie had just moved into had been bought with Molly in mind.

Alex appeared to have adjusted to being the baby's uncle instead of her father. He was just as attentive, and every bit as loving. Still, Grace struggled with a twinge of guilt as his wife got up to retrieve the stuffed turtle Molly had chucked out of her playpen.

"Tell me the truth," she said quietly when Julie dropped into her chair again. "Did Alex resent me for keeping my cousin's secret?"

"He did, for maybe a day or two after Blake showed him the final DNA results. He's a big boy, though. He worked through his disappointment." Her eyes took on a wicked glint. "I might have helped the process by redirecting his thoughts whenever I thought they needed it."

"Yes, I bet you… Oops, that's Blake's phone. He said something about expecting a call from Singapore. This may be it."

She scooped up the device he'd left on the table and checked caller ID. The number was a local one.

"Guess it's not Singapore."

Evidently the caller decided his message was too urgent to go to voice mail. Grace had no sooner set the phone down than it buzzed again, this time with a flashing icon indicating a text message.

"I'd better take this in to him. Keep an eye on Molly for me."

"Will do."

Phone in hand, she followed the sound of football fans in midroar to the den. Hoping it was the Dallas Cowboys who'd precipitated that roar, Grace shifted the phone to her other hand.

She honestly didn't mean to hit the text icon.

Or read the brief message that came up. But a single glance at the screen stopped her dead in her tracks.

Have an update on Petrie. Call me.

Ice crawled along Grace's veins. The hubbub in the den faded. The papered walls of the hall seemed to close in on her. She couldn't move, could barely breathe as Jack Petrie's image shoved everything else out of her mind. Smooth and handsome at first. Then smooth and sneering, as he was the last time he'd allowed Grace to visit his home. *His* home. Not her cousin's. Not one they'd made together. The house was his, the car was his, every friggin' dollar in the bank was his, to be doled out to *his* wife penny by penny.

The ice splintered. An almost forgotten fury now speared through Grace. Caught in its vicious maw, she let an animal cry rip from her throat and hurled the phone at the wall.

The Dalton men came running almost before the pieces hit the floor. Alex erupted from the den first.

"What the…?"

"Grace!" Blake shoved past his brother. "Are you okay?"

She didn't answer. *Couldn't* answer. Fury still clawed at her throat.

"Has something happened to Molly?" He gripped her upper arms. "Alex! Go check on Julie and the baby!"

He could have saved his breath. His brother was already pounding down the hall.

"Talk to me, Grace." Blake's fingers bit into her flesh. "Tell me what's happened."

"You got a call. That's what happened."

"What?"

She wrenched out of his hold. With a scathing look, she directed his attention to the shattered phone. He frowned at the pieces in obvious confusion.

"It was a text message." She fought to choke out the words. "My thumb hit the icon by mistake. I didn't intend to read the message. Wasn't intended to read it, obviously."

"What are you talking about? What message? Who was it from?"

"I'm guessing your friend, the P.I. What's his name? Jerrold? James?"

His jaw went tight. "Jamison."

"Right," she said venomously. "Jamison. He wants you to call him. For an update on Petrie."

"Oh, hell."

The soft expletive said it all. Spinning, Grace stalked down the hall and almost bowled over the two who emerged from the library. Any other time she might have noted with interest that a good portion of Delilah's crimson lipstick had transferred from her mouth to Dusty Jones's. At the moment all she could do was snap a curt response when Delilah demanded to know what was going on.

"Ask your son."

She brushed past them, wishing to hell she'd pocketed the keys to the snazzy new Jaguar Blake had insisted on buying her. She needed to get out. Think through this shock. But the keys were on the dresser. Upstairs. In the guest suite. Grace hit the stairs, grinding her teeth in mingled fury and frustration.

By the time she reached the luxuriously appointed suite, she'd added a searing sense of betrayal to the mix. She snatched the keys off the dresser, digging the jagged edges into her palm, staring unseeing at other objects scattered across the polished mahogany.

"Going somewhere?"

She jerked her head up and locked angry eyes on her husband. "I'm thinking about it."

"Mind if I ask where?" he asked calmly.

Too calmly, damn him! She'd always admired his steady thinking and cool composure. Not now. Not with this hurt knifing into her.

"I believed you," she threw at him. "When you said you could live with my refusal to betray Anne's trust, I actually believed you!"

"I am living with it."

"Like hell!"

His eyes narrowed but he kept his movements steady and unhurried as he turned, shut the door and faced her again.

"When you wouldn't trust me with Anne's secrets..."

"I couldn't! Some of us," she added viciously, "hold to our promises."

"When you *couldn't* trust me with Anne's secrets," he amended, his mouth thinning a little, "I had Jamison keep digging. I know now her real name was Hope Templeton."

The telltale signs that he was holding on to his temper with an effort took some of the edge off Grace's own anger. The hurt remained.

"I only had one cousin. Her birth is a matter of record. I'm surprised it took your hotshot P.I. so long to discover her real name."

"I also know she got married at the age of seventeen."

"How did you…? I mean, we…"

"Altered the record? I won't bother to remind you that's a crime."

He was in full lawyer mode now. Legs spread, arms crossed. Relentlessly presenting the evidence. The two of them would have to have this out, Grace realized. Once, and hopefully for all.

Reining in the last of her temper, she sank onto the bed. "Go on."

"What my hotshot P.I. did not find was any record of divorce. I can only assume Anne was still married when she and I met. I can also assume the marriage wasn't a happy one."

"And how did you reach this brilliant deduction?"

He shrugged aside the sarcasm. "The fact that Anne had left him, obviously. And that she used an assumed name, presumably to prevent him from finding her."

Grace could add so much more to the list. Like Anne's aversion to public places for fear Petrie or one of his friends would spot her. Her bone-deep distrust of all men until this one. Her abrupt disappearance from Blake's life, even though she must have loved him.

"I had Jamison check out her husband," he said, breaking into the dark, sad memories. "According to Texas Highway Patrol records, Jack Petrie is a highly decorated officer with two citations for risking his life in the line of duty. One for dragging a man and his son out of a burning vehicle. Another for taking down a drug smuggler who shot a fellow officer during a routine traffic stop."

"You didn't contact him, did you?" Grace asked with her heart in her throat.

"No. Neither did Jamison. But he made discreet inquiries."

She breathed in, out. "And?"

"Jamison came away with the impression Petrie was a devoted husband who liked to show off his pretty young wife. Rumor has it he was devastated when she walked out on him."

Blake waited for her to deny the rumor. When she didn't, he got to the real issue. "That leaves Molly."

"She's your child, Blake!" The exclamation burst out, quick and passionate. "Not Petrie's!"

"I know that. Even without the DNA evidence, Jamison's sources confirmed Anne left her husband almost a year before she and I met. Still, they were married when she gave birth to Molly, and under the law..."

"To hell with the law! You've run the tests. If it ever came to a legal battle, you've got more than enough evidence to support your paternity."

She came off the bed, pleading now.

"But it doesn't need come to a battle. Anne's dead. Petrie has no idea she had a child. Just leave it that way."

"What are you so afraid of, Grace? What was Anne afraid of? Did Petrie hurt her? Use his fists on her?"

"I..."

"Tell me, for God's sake!"

She almost broke down then. She would have given her soul at that point to share the whole, degrading truth, but her promise hung like an anchor around her neck. All she would respond to was one specific question.

"It wasn't physical. Not that I know of, anyway. But mental cruelty can be just as vicious."

"All the more reason for me to protect Molly from this jerk."

He had the training, the extensive network of connections to enact all sorts of legal sanctions. She knew that. She also knew the mere fact he'd had an affair with Anne would drive Jack Petrie to a jealous rage. The man was a sadist. He'd strangled his wife with a warped kind of love that others mistook for devotion. Anne was beyond his reach now, but her child wasn't. Or her lover.

"You've just proved my point," Grace countered with a touch of desperation. "You think

Anne's husband won't want vengeance? He'll try to milk you for millions. Drag a paternity suit out in court for years. Have you thought of that?"

"Of course," he snapped. "I'm not afraid of a fight, legal or otherwise."

Okay. All right. She had to breathe deep. Slow down. Remember she wasn't dealing with someone as unbalanced as Jack Petrie.

"Put your own feelings aside for a moment, Blake. Think what a long, drawn-out court battle could do to Molly. When she's older she'll be curious about her mother. All she'd have to do is surf the Net. You can imagine the headlines she'll stumble across. Billionaire's Love Child Center of Vicious Paternity Dispute. Decorated Police Officer Calls Wife a Whore. Secretary Hooks Rich Boss with Sex And…"

"I've got the picture."

He got it, and he didn't like it. She didn't, either, but they couldn't ignore it.

"Don't dig any further, Blake. Please! In a year, two years, everyone outside our immediate circle will just assume Molly's our child. Petrie won't have any reason to question it."

He looked as if she'd punched him in the gut. Or square in his sense of right and wrong. His eyes went cold, his voice flat and hard.

"So you want to live a lie. Like your cousin."

For Molly's sake she gave the only answer she could. "Yes."

Twelve

"She just can't bring herself to trust me."

Blake gripped his beer and ignored the buzz from the crowd gathered in the watering spot a few blocks from Dalton International's corporate headquarters. He and his brother had wrapped a bitch of a meeting with senior executives from Nippon Steel earlier that evening, then taken their Japanese visitors to dinner at one of Oklahoma City's finest steak houses. The Nippon execs had taken a limo back to their hotel, leaving Blake and Alex to lick their wounds over a beer and a bucket of peanuts before heading home to their respective spouses. Despite the round of tough negotiations, it was Blake's spouse who occupied his mind more than the Japanese.

"I accept that Grace promised to keep Anne's secrets," he said, stretching his long legs out beneath a tabletop littered with peanut shells. "I respect her for holding to that vow, but Christ! We've been married almost a month now and she still doesn't think I can handle this character Petrie."

Shrugging, Alex attempted to take the middle road on the subject he and his twin had already beaten into the ground a number of times. "Grace knows Petrie. We don't."

"We know enough! The bastard terrorized his wife and forced her into a shadow life. Now he's doing the same thing to *my* wife."

Frustration ate like acid at Blake's gut. It was doing a serious number on his pride, too. He yanked at the knot of his tie and popped the top button of his shirt before downing a slug of beer.

"Mother says Grace stays in the background at the charity functions she's involved her in and ducks whenever a photographer shows up. She does the same when we attend a concert or some black-tie affair. The woman is fixated on maintaining a low profile until our marriage is old news."

"So? You don't exactly chase after the spotlight yourself."

"Dammit, bro, you're not helping here."

"You wanted a sounding board, I'm doing my best board act." Peanut shells crunched as his twin leaned his elbows on the table. "I've told you what I really think."

"Yeah, I know. You think I should take a quick trip to San Antonio and confront this guy. Let him know who he'd be dealing with if he got any smart ideas."

"Correction. I think *we* should take a quick trip to San Antonio."

"It's my problem! I'll handle it."

"You're doing a helluva job with it so far."

Blake's lips drew back in a snarl. He managed to choke it off. Barely. Alex knew damned well he was spoiling for a fight. Obviously, his twin was prepared to step in and draw the punches.

"Well, at least you've got Jamison's sources keeping an eye on Petrie," Alex commented.

"I'm getting regular updates."

"Does Grace know?"

"She knows."

That had caused another rough scene. Grace argued that Petrie was a cop. Sooner or later he would pick up on a surveillance, become suspicious, track it to the source. Blake countered with the assertion that Jamison and his associate in San Antonio were pros. They wouldn't tip their hands. In either case, Blake flatly refused to turn a blind eye to a potential threat.

Grace had conceded that point. Reluctantly, but she'd conceded. Still, the fact they were living with this guy Petrie's shadow hanging over them locked Blake's jaw every time he thought about it. He'd promised his wife he wouldn't confront the man without talking it over with her first. That discussion was fast approaching. In the meantime, he and Grace each pretended they understood and accepted the other's viewpoint.

"I get that Grace saw firsthand the hell Petrie put her cousin through," Alex said, attacking the matter from another angle. "What I don't get is why she doesn't want to take him on. I didn't know Anne all that well, but I do know Grace. My sense is she's much stronger than her cousin was."

"Stronger, and a whole bunch more stubborn," Blake agreed with a grimace.

"She's also got us to do the muscle work. All of us. Mother and Julie want in on this. Dusty, too."

Momentarily diverted, Blake raised a brow. "Yeah, what's with that? The old coot's at Mom's house just about every time I stop by there these days."

"They're consulting," Alex replied, deadpan. "As Julie's business partner and coowner of one of Dalton International's subsidiaries, Dusty prefers to talk shop with someone who worked the same oil patches he did."

"Oh, Lord! I'm not going to tell you the image that just jumped into my head. But..." Blake raised his beer. "Here's to 'em."

Grinning, the brothers clinked bottles. Alex signaled the waitress to bring two fresh ones before returning to the issue digging at them both.

"Back to Grace. She's got to know she can

count on you, on all of us, to protect her from this asshole Petrie."

"She knows," Blake said grimly. "The problem is she thinks she's protecting us. Or Molly and me, anyway."

His brother winced. "That's got to stick in your craw."

"Like you wouldn't believe."

He didn't go into further detail. As a kid Alex had been the one to wade fist-first into battle. Blake had always had his brother's back, though, and Alex his. The fact that his wife didn't trust him to have hers rubbed him raw. Feeling the grate yet again, he circled his beer bottle on the littered table and sent a shower of peanut shells to the already carpeted floor.

"So how long are you going to play this by her rules?" Alex wanted to know.

Blake's head snapped up. The uncompromising answer came fast. "The rules change the moment I sense so much as a hint of a real threat."

Grace was perched on one of the kitchen counter stools when she heard the muted rumble of the garage door going up. She'd put Molly down for the night at seven-thirty and indulged in the sybaritic luxury of an hour-long soak in scented bath oil that evoked instant memories of Provence's hot sun and endless lavender fields. Barefoot and supremely comfortable in a well-washed, black-and-silver San Antonio Spurs jersey that came almost to her knees, she'd curled up with a biography of Van Gogh before deciding to treat herself to a bowl of double chocolate fudge ripple. After so many years of busy days in the classroom and nights grading papers, she loved having the time and the freedom to read whatever struck her fancy. She loved even more reading to Molly, which she'd started doing before they'd moved into the house Grace was having such fun furnishing.

All in all, her days were perfect. The nights came pretty darn close.

Grace had gotten past her anger over Blake directing his P.I. to dig into the past her cousin had tried so desperately to escape. She'd also recovered—mostly—from the stinging sense of betrayal that he'd done it after she'd begged him to let that past stay buried. She understood his rationale. She didn't agree with it, but she understood it.

Unfortunately, a difference of opinion on something so crucial couldn't help but affect their continually evolving relationship. The strain it had caused was like a small but irritating itch they'd mutually decided to ignore.

Despite the itch, they still took pleasure in discovering new facets to each other's personalities. The quirks, the unconscious gestures, the ingrained habits. What's more, they still shared the sheer joy of Molly. And Grace's pulse still bumped whenever her husband walked into a room.

Like now. She swiveled the stool, cradling her bowl of double chocolate fudge ripple, and felt the flutter as Blake entered the kitchen through the utility room connected to the garage. He moved with the athletic ease she so admired and looked as classy as ever, although the open shirt collar and the tie dangling from his suit coat pocket added a definite touch of sex to the sophisticated image.

They hadn't reached the stage of casual, hello-honey-I'm-home kisses yet. Grace wasn't sure they ever would, although she knew darn well they couldn't sustain indefinitely the searing heat they'd ignited during their honeymoon. She felt it sizzle now, though, as he nudged her knees apart so he could stand between them and cupped her nape.

"Did you and Alex get your Japanese execs all wined and dined?"

"We did."

His palm was warm against her skin, his eyes a smoky blue as his head bent toward hers. Tipping her chin, Grace welcomed him home with a kiss that left her breathless and Blake demanding a second one just like the first. She gave both willingly, as greedy as he was, but had to jerk back when the fudge ripple threatened to slide into her lap.

Blake eyed the bowl's contents with interest. "That looks good."

"Sit down, I'll get you some."

"I'll just share yours."

"Hmmmm." Her brow furrowed in a mock

scowl. "In the 'just for future reference' category, I don't usually share my ice cream. Or my fries."

"Noted. But you'll make an exception in this instance, right?"

Since he was still wedged between her thighs and didn't look as though he planned to move anytime soon, she yielded the point.

"Okay. Here you go."

He downed the heaping spoonful in one try, prompting a quick warning.

"Whoa! You'll get a brain freeze gobbling it down like that."

A slow, predatory smile curved his mouth. "No part of me is liable to freeze like this."

He moved closer, spreading her wider. The Spurs jersey rode up, and Grace felt him harden against her.

"I see what you mean," she got out on a gasp when he exerted an exquisite pressure at the juncture of her thighs. "No danger of frost down there."

Or anywhere else!

The pressure increased. The muscles low in her belly clenched. He splayed his hands on her

hips to keep her anchored, and the wild, throb-
bing sensation built with each rhythmic move of
his lower body against hers.

"Blake!" She tried to wiggle away but the counter dug into her back. "We'd better slow down. I
can't... You've got me too..."

"Hold on."

Like she could? Especially when he spanned
her waist and lifted her in a smooth, easy move
from the stool to the counter. She didn't even realize she still held the now-melted ice cream until
he took the bowl and let it clatter into the sink.
Then the jersey came up and over her head. Her
bikini briefs got peeled off. Her mouth was level
with his now, her hips in line with his belt. She
should have felt completely, nakedly exposed.
All she experienced was the urgent need to get
him naked, too.

"Your jacket... Shirt..."

He shed the top half of his clothing with mini-
mum movement and maximum speed. The bottom half stayed intact as he buried a fist in her
hair, and took her mouth with his.

There was something different in this kiss, in the maddening pressure he exerted against her. He was a little rougher, a little harder, yet somehow more deliberate. As though he could demonstrate some sort of mastery over her if he wanted to but chose to restrain himself. Or not. Grace didn't register more than that hazy impression before he replaced his lower body with his hand and drove everything resembling rational thought out of her head.

She came mere moments later in a burst of bright colors and pure sensation. The explosive climax arched her spine and brought her head back. She slapped her palms on the counter to support her taut, shuddering body, but her arms folded like overstretched elastic.

Blake scooped her off the counter before she went horizontal and carried her limp and still quivering with pleasure to the bedroom. When he shed the rest of his clothes and joined her in bed for the grand finale, he was so gentle and tender Grace completely forgot that odd moment in the kitchen.

* * *

It came back with a vengeance less than a week later.

Yielding to her mother-in-law's indomitable will, she strapped Molly into her car seat to drive her over to the Nichols Hills mansion for some grandmother-granddaughter time. Grace herself had been instructed to shop for a cocktail dress for the big-dollar fundraiser Delilah insisted her sons and their wives attend the following evening.

"Which I really do *not* want to go to," she said via the rearview mirror to the infant happily banging a teething ring against the side window.

Her eyes on the baby, she had to jam on the brakes to avoid an SUV cruising past the end of the drive. The near miss rattled Grace and reminded her to keep her attention on the road. The brief visit with Delilah didn't exactly soothe her somewhat frayed nerves.

"You should get your nails done while you're out," her mother-in-law suggested after a prolonged exchange of Eskimo kisses with a joyously squealing Molly. "Your hair trimmed, too."

"I look that bad, huh?"

"You look gorgeous and you know it." She hitched the baby on her hip and skewered her daughter-in-law with one of her rapier stares. "Just not as glowing as you did when you got back from Provence. Don't tell me you and Blake have taken the sex down a notch already."

"I won't," Grace countered coolly.

"Don't get on your high horse with me, girl. If it's not sex, it has to be that business with Jamison. Look, I don't like to meddle in my sons' lives but..."

She paused and waited with a reluctant grin for Grace to finish snorting.

"Okay, okay. Meddling is my favorite occupation. But I thought you and Blake had come to an understanding on that matter."

"We have. More or less."

The older woman let Molly play with her sapphire-and-diamond wrist bangle and skinned Grace with another serrated look. "I'm only going to say this once. I'll never mention it again, I swear."

Grace believed that as much as she believed her

former employer could keep her nose out of her sons' affairs. Once Delilah got the bit between her teeth, she kept it there.

"You did right standing by your promise to your cousin," she said, "but she's dead and you're married now. You need to decide where your loyalty lies."

Grace went rigid, her eyes flashing danger signals. They bounced off Delilah's thick hide.

"Go," she ordered brusquely. "Shop, have your nails done, and for God's sake think about what I just said."

Grace fumed all the way to the exclusive boutique she and Julie had discovered some months ago. She pulled into a parking slot two doors down and killed the Jag's engine, then sat with her fists gripping the leather-wrapped steering wheel.

She didn't need Delilah to lecture her about loyalty, dammit! She'd spent what felt like half her life and every penny of her income shielding Anne from her sadistic husband. If she closed her eyes, she could still see her cousin fighting desperately for her last breaths. Hear her rasping plea for Grace to take Molly to her father and please, *please* don't let Jack know about her.

Her knuckles whitened on the wheel. She stared at the shop window in front of the Jag. The window was bare except for a For Lease sign, but Grace barely noticed the empty expanse of glass and darkened interior.

Maybe...

Maybe the habit of protecting her cousin had become too ingrained. Maybe she'd been following instincts tainted by Anne's bone-deep fear when she should be trusting Blake's. He was calm and cool in a crisis. And more intelligent than any six people she knew. He could also wield resources every bit as if not more powerful than Jack Petrie's. Most important, he was Molly's father. He'd strangle anyone who tried to harm her with his bare hands.

Groaning, Grace dropped her forehead to the wheel. Heart and soul, she ached to hold to the promise she made her cousin. She couldn't. Not any longer. Delilah was right. She had to let go of Anne's past. Her future revolved around Molly and Blake. With a silent plea to her cousin to understand, she raised her head and fumbled in her purse for her cell phone.

She pressed one speed-dial key. Her husband's superefficient executive assistant answered before the second ring.

"Blake Dalton's office."

"Hi, Patrice, it's Grace. Is Blake free?"

"Hi, Grace. Sorry, but he's in the middle of a conference call with the Association of Corporate Counsel's executive committee. They want him to chair the next symposium, you know."

"Yes, I do."

"Shall I pass him a note to let him know you're on the line?"

"No, just tell him… Tell him I was thinking about my cousin and…"

Hell! She couldn't put what she wanted to say on a yellow call slip.

"Just tell him I called."

"I will."

"Thanks."

She tapped End, feeling much like Julius Caesar must have when he brought his legionnaires across the Rubicon. She couldn't go back now. She didn't *want* to go back. She'd charge full steam ahead with Blake and Molly and a life without the specter of Jack Petrie hanging over it.

She was still riding the relief of that decision when she emerged from Helen Jasper's boutique some time later. As usual, the shop owner's eye had proved as unerring as her taste. She'd purchased the entire line of a young Oklahoma designer she was sure would make a splash in the fashion world. Grace ended up buying not only a tea-length cocktail dress in dreamy shades of green, but two beaded tops and a pair of slinky palazzo pants with accessories to match. She'd also had Helen bundle up the outfit she'd worn into the store and now felt very autumnal in heavyweight linen slacks in cinnamon-brown, a matching tank top and a pumpkin-colored silk overblouse left unbuttoned to show off a faux lizardskin belt as wide, if not as clanky, as Delilah's.

Smiling at the thought of Blake's reaction to the backless and darned near frontless cocktail dress, she bunched her shopping bags in one hand

and fumbled in her purse for the car keys. She popped the door locks, dropped her purse on the front seat and was about to add the shopping bags when a black SUV wheeled into the slot next to hers. The idiot driver cut into the space so sharply she had to quickly yank on the open door to avoid having it dinged.

Mentally giving him the bird, she bent to retrieve the tissue-stuffed bags her quick move had sent tumbling to the floor mat. When she straightened, she caught a glimpse of the other driver from the corner of one eye. He'd exited his vehicle but hadn't moved away from it.

A prickly sense of unease raced along her spine. He was standing close to her Jag. Too close. A half dozen tips from the various self-defense articles she'd read crowded into her mind. She went with the only one she could.

Jamming her car keys between her fingers, she closed her fist to form a spiked gauntlet and started to turn. She didn't get even halfway around before something hard rammed against her shoulder blade and her world turned red.

Thirteen

"She doesn't answer her phone."

Blake paced his brother's office on the twentieth floor of Dalton International's headquarters. Wall-to-wall windows offered a different perspective of downtown Oklahoma City than that in his own office at the opposite end of the long corridor bisecting the CEO's suites. But Blake had no interest in the sweeping panorama of the round-domed capitol building in the distance or the colorful barges meandering along the river in the foreground. He took another few paces, his fists jammed in the pocket of his slacks.

"I've left three voice mails. The first was around ten-thirty, the last one a half hour ago."

Although it was now just a little past two, Alex understood his brother's concern. He'd spent several tense hours himself when Julie took off in search of a missing Dusty Jones, her cell phone died and Alex didn't know where the hell she'd disappeared to. When he reminded Blake of that knuckle-cracking episode, his brother shook his head.

"I thought of that, but her phone was sitting in the charger next to mine when I left the house this morning. It's fully juiced."

"And Mother didn't know where Grace was heading?"

"Not specifically. Just that she was going shopping and maybe to get her hair or nails done."

"That sure narrows it down," Alex said drily as he reached for the phone on the broad plane of his desk. "I'll call Julie. I remember her mentioning some boutique or other that she and Grace really like."

Luckily, he caught his wife on the ground between crop-dusting runs. Julie had come to a reluctant decision to quit flying agro-air, worried that its high concentration of chemicals could affect the baby she and Alex had decided to try for. She was in the process of training a replacement now—and acclimating the poor guy to the challenges and dubious joys of working with Dusty.

Blake tried to suppress his nagging worry while his brother explained the situation to his wife and scribbled a couple of numbers on a notepad before promising to call back once they'd located Grace.

"She said to try a boutique owned by a woman named Helen Jasper." Alex punched in the first number. "Also a nail salon on... Hello? Ms. Jasper? This is Alex Dalton."

He listened a moment and smiled.

"Yes, I am. Very lucky. So is my brother. That's why I'm calling, actually. We need to get in touch with Grace, but her cell phone's not working. She was going shopping, and Julie said to try your place." His glance cut to Blake. "She did? All right, thanks."

Some of the tension riding Blake's shoulders left when Alex reported his wife had spent several hours and what sounded like a big chunk of change in the boutique.

"She left a little before noon. Maybe she stopped somewhere for a leisurely lunch."

"Maybe." The tension ratcheted up again. "But I can't see her lingering over a long lunch without calling to check on Molly."

"Let's try this nail place. She could have…"

Alex broke off, frowning when the door to his office opened. His executive assistant sent him an apologetic look as Delilah swept in pushing Molly's stroller, unannounced as usual. The matriarch of the Dalton clan—and nominal president of DI's board of directors—saw no reason why she had to wait for an underling to grant her access to either of her sons.

She halted the stroller in front of Blake. "Your assistant said you were here with Alex."

He barely had time to absorb her knee-high boots, black leggings and rust-colored tunic cinched with a monster leather belt decorated with an assortment of dangling, clinking zoo animals in silver and gold before Molly gave a joyous screech.

"Da-da!"

His heart turning over, Blake responded to his daughter's outstretched arms by unclipping the stroller's safety belt and gathering her in his. She brought with her that ever-fascinating, always changing combination of baby smells. Today it was powder and strained peaches and a faint, yeasty scent he couldn't identify.

"Have you heard from Grace?" Delilah demanded while Molly planted wet kisses on his cheek.

"No, but we know she left her favorite boutique a couple of hours ago."

"I was just saying she may be treating herself to a late lunch," Alex put in.

"She wouldn't do that," Delilah asserted flatly. "Not without giving me a call first to check on Molly."

The skin at the back of Blake's neck stretched taut. His mother had just confirmed his own thoughts.

"Patrice said Grace left a message for you earlier," she continued. "She didn't communicate her plans for the rest of the day?"

"Just that she wanted me to call her."

"That's it?"

"No." Blake's jaw tightened. "After she didn't reply to my second voice message, I grilled Patrice. She said Grace mentioned wanting to talk about her cousin, then changed her mind and just asked Patrice to tell me she called."

"Her cousin?"

Despite the distraction of Molly's palm slapping his cheek, he didn't miss the sudden flicker of guilt in his mother's eyes.

"What do you know that I don't?"

"Well…"

With a sudden premonition of disaster, Blake passed Molly across the desk to her uncle and locked on his mother. "Tell me what you did."

"I didn't *do* anything," she huffed. "I merely suggested to my daughter-in-law that she might want to think about whether she owes her loyalty to her dead cousin or her very much alive family."

"Dammit! I told you not to interfere in this."

"You're raising a daughter," she fired back. "You should know by now that being a parent gives you the inalienable right to interfere when necessary."

Too furious to counter that broadside, Blake strode to the windows. He knew damned well that Grace *did* think about where her loyalty lay. Continuously. The matter twisted her in as many knots as it did him.

Had she gotten fed up with the pressure he and now Delilah had put on her? Was that why she hadn't responded to his return calls? Had she decided she needed some downtime, away from the Daltons, mother and son?

Christ! Would she just disappear? Walk out of his life as Anne had?

The thought put a hard, fast kink in his gut. Just as fast, Blake unkinked it. There was no way Grace would do that to him. She had too much integrity, too strong a sense of fair play. They'd argued over this whole mess, sure, but she knew he loved her too much to let her just disappear from his life.

Didn't she?

Brought up short, he tried to remember if he'd articulated the actual words. Maybe not, but he'd sure as hell showed her how he felt. The fact that he couldn't keep his hands off her spoke louder than words. As if it were an implied-in-fact contract, the attorney in him asserted, she could certainly infer his feelings from his actions.

Right, the less legalistic side of his mind sneered. Just as he could now infer why she hadn't returned his calls.

Well, there was one possible reason he could address right now. Cell phone in hand, he brought up the address book and hit Jamison's number.

"It's Blake Dalton," he said tersely. "I need an update on Petrie."

"Got a report a half hour ago," the P.I. informed him. "I was just going to email it to you."

"Give me the gist."

"Hang on, let me pull it up. Okay, here it is. Electronic surveillance of Petrie's residence showed him returning there yesterday afternoon at fourteen-thirty hours. My associate checked with his source in his highway patrol unit. Petrie and his partner testified in court in the morning. Reportedly, he felt queasy afterward, said he was coming down with something. He took the rest of the day off and called in for sick leave again this morning, saying he had a doctor's appointment. Surveillance showed him leaving his residence in civilian clothes at oh-six-fifteen."

Blake's eyes narrowed. "Pretty early for a doctor's appointment."

"That's what I thought, too. I've got my guy digging deeper."

"Call me as soon as... Wait. Back up a minute. You said Petrie testified in court yesterday morning?"

"Right. On a drug-stop case that crossed state lines and involved the feds. I've got the specifics here if you..."

"I don't need the specifics. Just tell me which court."

"Bexar County, 73rd Judicial District," Jamison reported after a moment. "Judge Honeywell presiding."

It might not mean anything. Honeywell heard dozens of cases every week. But the possibility, however remote, that Petrie might have picked up something about Grace from the judge or his assistant put the crimp back in Blake's gut.

"Call your associate in San Antonio. Tell him to put everything he's got on this. I want him to know Petrie's exact whereabouts, like fast."

"Will do."

He palmed the phone and was just turning to update the others when Alex's intercom buzzed. Shifting Molly to his right arm, his twin reached for the phone. Blake felt a surge of hope that Patrice had forwarded a call from Grace to his brother's office. That hope sank like a stone when Alex flashed him a quick frown.

"Yes, I'll take the call." He jiggled Molly, waited a moment and identified himself. "This is Alex Dalton."

Blake cut across the office. He pressed against the front edge of Alex's desk as the groove between his twin's brows dug deeper.

"Right. Thanks for calling."

"What?" Blake demanded before Alex had dropped the instrument back on the hook.

"That was Helen Jasper, the woman who owns the boutique where Grace shopped this morning. She just went out for a late lunch break and spotted Grace's car parked a couple doors down from her shop."

His voice was as grim as his face.

"She looked in the Jag's window. Said she could see the bags from her store spilling off the front passenger seat. Grace's purse is on the floor with them."

Delilah took Molly back to her house while her sons set out across town. Alex navigated, and Blake drove with a fierce concentration that was only minimally directed at the road. He tried to tell himself there were a number of reasons Grace might have left the Jag parked outside the boutique for so long. But none of reasons he dredged up explained her leaving her purse inside, in full view of anyone tempted to smash a window and empty it of wallet and credit cards.

"There's the boutique," Alex said when Blake pulled into the parking lot of an upscale strip mall. "And there's Grace's Jag."

Blake screeched into a slot beside the midnight-blue sedan and jammed his own vehicle into Park. He carried a spare key to the Jag on his key ring and was aiming it to beep the locks when Alex put out a restraining hand.

"There could be fingerprints or fibers or other evidence."

Like blood. He didn't say it. He didn't have to.

"Sure you want to contaminate the scene?"

"I've driven this car dozens of times. My prints, clothing fibers and DNA are all over it, but I'll be careful."

As it turned out, the doors weren't locked. Blake used the underside of the handle to open one. The baby seat sat empty in the back with some of Molly's toys scattered beside it. The front passenger seat held a jumble of shopping bags. Additional bags had obviously tumbled off the seat onto the floor. Grace's purse lay half-buried amid the silver tissue paper and pale blue bags. Her cell phone was clearly visible in the purse's side pocket.

Jaw clenched, Blake moved to the rear of the vehicle and used the key to pop the trunk. His breath escaped in a hiss of sheer relief when he found it empty. Alex gave him a silent, sympathetic thump on the shoulder. Blake knew he'd imagined the worst, too, although the empty trunk provided only temporary respite from those grim scenarios.

"I'll call Harkins," Alex said curtly.

Phil Harkins was a friend as well as a supremely competent chief of police. Alex had his phone out when Blake yanked on his arm.

"Wait!"

He ducked under the raised trunk lid and came back up with a half-folded sheet of paper he'd missed on the first, anxious sweep. The message inside was scrawled in bold black ink.

You took my wife. I took yours. If you want to see the bitch alive again, you'd better keep this between you and me. A rich prick like you shouldn't have much trouble finding us. We'll be waiting for you.

Blake swore savagely and passed the note to Alex. His brother was still reading it when Blake's cell phone pinged. He checked caller ID, saw it was Jamison and cut right to the chase.

"What have you got?"

"Petrie flew out of San Antonio on a oh-seven-ten flight direct to Oklahoma City. He landed at eight-twenty, picked up one checked bag and rented a black Chevy Traverse from Hertz, Oklahoma tag six-three-two-delta-hotel-eight."

"Does the rental have a vehicle-tracking device?" Blake bit out.

"It does, but Hertz wouldn't give me access to their system."

"I'll take care of that."

He skimmed his contacts and pulled up Phil Harkins's number. The DA was in his office, thank God.

"Hey, pardner," he said with the affable geniality he showed to everyone except the worst of the bottom feeders his office prosecuted. "How's it hanging?"

"I need a favor, Phil. Fast, with no questions asked."

"Shoot."

Ten nerve-twisting minutes later, Harkins delivered.

"Hertz just transmitted the GPS tracking data.

Your boy departed the airport, drove to your neighborhood and cruised your street. Didn't stop, but made a sharp U-turn at nine-fifty-four and drove to Nichols Hills."

Hell! He'd been following Grace. Blake was sure of it.

"He idled a block from your mother's place for eighteen minutes," Harkins recited, "then drove to your present location, where he sat for almost two hours."

Watching Helen Jasper's boutique. Waiting for Grace.

"Do your people have a lock on him now?" Blake asked, his insides ice-cold.

"Roger. He's heading south on I-35, three miles from the Texas border." Harkins hesitated. "I don't know what you have going on here, but I can ask the Texas Highway Patrol to make a stop."

Blake couldn't chance it. Petrie was a Texas state trooper. He could have his radio with him and be listening in on their net.

"No, don't alert the troopers. Just keep tracking

him and let me know if he deviates from I-35."
He shot his brother a fast look. "I'll be in the air."

Alex was punching the speed call number for his chief of air operations before Blake disconnected.

"What have we got ready to go?" He listened then issued a terse instruction. "Top off the fuel tank on the Skylane. We'll be there in fifteen minutes."

Blake didn't question the choice of a single-engine turboprop over one of Dalton International's bigger, faster corporate jets. Alex could put the Skylane down in a cow pasture if he had to.

They were in the air less than a half hour later. Alex laid on max airspeed and made a swift calculation.

"We should catch them between Austin and San Antonio…if that's where the bastard's headed."

Blake nodded, his eyes shielded by the sunglasses he'd put on to protect them from the unfiltered sunlight. He kept his narrowed, intent gaze trained on the wide ribbon of concrete cutting across the rolling hills and checkered fields below.

Petrie was down there, a thousand feet below and almost two hours ahead, driving a black Chevy Traverse. Blake could only pray he'd stuck to his end of the deal and had Grace sitting alive and unhurt beside him.

Fourteen

Grace shifted in the bucket seat, biting down hard on her lip when the SUV jounced over a rut. With her arms cuffed behind her, the ache between her shoulder blades had magnified to sheer torture in the interminable hour since she'd regained consciousness.

She turned her face to the window to hide a wince and searched for a landmark, any kind of a landmark. All she could see was a dense forest of stunted live oaks poking above an impenetrable wall of scrub. Refusing to give in to the desperation squeezing her chest like a vise, she faced front again and forced herself to speak coolly.

"Where are we going?"

Buzz-cut, tanned and clean-shaven, the out-wardly all-American guy in the driver's seat wrenched his gaze from the single-lane dirt road ahead and shot her a look of smiling malevolence.

"I told you. You'll know when we get there. Now unless you want to talk to me about that rich bastard who screwed my wife…"

Grace set her jaw.

"That's okay, cuz. You'll be squealing soon enough. Now shut the hell up. I don't want to miss the turn."

This was how it had gone since Grace had come to, dizzy and nauseous and aching all over. Petrie had refused to tell her how he'd found her. Refused to do more than smile with amused contempt when Grace warned he wouldn't get away with snatching her off the street.

She knew without being told that kidnapping wasn't all he intended. He was a cop. He wouldn't leave a live victim to bring him down. She also knew he intended to use her as bait to get to Blake.

She'd been so careful! How had he made the

connection between Blake and Anne? No, not Anne! Hope! She had to think of her cousin as Hope again, use that name when referring to her, or she'd feed into the rage smoldering behind Petrie's careful facade.

Ten minutes later Grace caught a glimpse of blue water through the screen of trees. Five minutes more, and Petrie slowed to a near crawl, then turned onto an overgrown dirt track. Grace had no idea how he spotted the track. There was no mailbox, no scrap of cloth tied to a bush, nothing but two sunken ruts cutting through the heavy underbrush.

Thorny vines and ranches scraped the SUV's sides. He was doing one helluva number on the paint job, she thought with vicious satisfaction, then gritted her teeth as the SUV bounced over the ruts and white-hot needles stabbed into her aching shoulders. She wanted to sob with relief when the brush finally thinned and the dirt track gave onto a clearing that sloped down to a good-size lake.

A cedar-shingled cabin sat at the top of the slope, well above the waterline. Cinder blocks supported a screened-in porch. Additional cinder blocks formed columns to hold up the roof that shaded the porch. Grace whipped her gaze from the cabin to tree-studded opposite shore and spotted two or three similar structures. Most looked as if they were boarded up. None was within screaming distance.

Petrie pulled well off the track, killed the engine and got out. Leaving his door open, he extracted something from the floor behind his seat. A rifle case, Grace saw. Hand-tooled leather. Padded handle. Housing for the high-powered hunting rifle she'd seen him clean at his kitchen table more than once.

The case terrified her. Not for herself. For Blake. He would come after her. Find her somehow. Walk right into Petrie's gun sight.

The terror spiked again when Petrie got out and propped the rifle against the fender before extracting a soft-sided pistol case from his door's side bin. The case was half-zipped, providing easy access to the blue steel semiautomatic he slid out. It wasn't his service weapon. Grace had seen his state-issued black leather holster and Sig

Sauer often enough to recognize the difference. This had to be a throwaway, one of those weapons reportedly confiscated during traffic stops that somehow never made it into evidence logs. Untraceable to the man who now coolly ejected the magazine and checked to verify a round was chambered before snapping the magazine back in place and thumbing the safety lock.

Just as coolly, he settled the pistol in the waistband of his jeans and picked up the rifle case. Grace's heart was racing when he rounded the hood, yanked open the passenger door and popped her seat belt.

"Let's go."

He hooked a hand around her upper arm and dragged her out, firing the pain in her shoulders to white-hot agony. It took every ounce of will she had not to moan as he hauled her up to the cabin. The screen door screeched when Petrie pulled it open, then groped above the main door for the key he obviously knew was there.

When he shoved Grace inside, the stink of old, dank blankets and used fishing tackle hit like a slap to the face. Grimacing, she inspected the dim interior. Bunk beds lined one wall. A rough-plank picnic table, a worn sofa with mismatched cushions and a lumpy armchair took up most of the remaining floorspace. The kitchen consisted of a counter with a sink, hot plate and half-size fridge. An unpainted door hung on its hinges at the far end of the room and gave a glimpse into a cubbyhole of a bathroom.

"Nice place you got here," Grace commented with a credible sneer.

"Belongs to a friend of mine. He's invited me up here a couple times to fish and drink. I know it offends your delicate sensibilities, but it'll do fine for what I have in mind, cuz."

"Stop calling me that, you dog turd. You and I are in no way related, thank God."

"You always were the feisty one."

She didn't like the slow, up-and-down look he gave her.

"I might just have to train you to heel, like I did Hope."

"You want to bet that's gonna happen?"

The face her cousin had once rhapsodized

about being so strong and stamped with character now radiated nothing but amused contempt.

"We'll see how full of piss and vinegar you are
when I'm done with you."

Dragging her across the room, he spun her so
she was nose to nose with the rolled-up mattress
on one of the top bunks. She felt him working the
cuffs on her left wrist, felt it spring free and the
screaming agony when her arm dropped to her
side. She knew she had only three or four seconds
to whirl and claw and fight for her freedom, but
before she could do more than curl her numbed
fingers Petrie had spun her around again. In a
quick move he snapped the free end of the cuff to
the metal pole supporting the upper bunk. Steel
rattled against steel as the cuff shimmied down
the pole.

"Make yourself comfortable, cuz. I figure
we've got some time before the fun starts."

With unhurried calm, he placed the tooled
leather case on the table, unzipped it and began
to assemble his hunting rifle.

Grace watched him, her arms dangling uselessly
at her sides. They felt as though they'd parted

company with her aching shoulders. When the blood finally pulsed back into them, she angled around as far as the cuff would allow and yanked at the rolled-up mattress on the lower bunk.

"All right, Jack," she said after she sank onto the dank ticking. "You may as well tell me. I know you're itching to rub my face in it."

"How I found you, you mean? Or how I found out about my whore of a wife and the rich dick you married?"

"Both."

"Took some doing," he admitted as he snapped the rifle's bolt into place. "I've been searching ever since Hope walked out on me. Checking state and county court records, making calls to various police departments, screening NamUS—the National Missing Persons Data System," he clarified gratuitously.

Grace knew damned well what NamUS was. The data system was open to anyone with a computer. She'd screened it regularly herself for updates on her cousin.

"It wasn't until your marriage license popped in the Texas Vital Statistics database that I finally got a solid lead, though. I saw Judge Honeywell had married you and talked up his assistant. She gushed about what a handsome couple you'd made, how the judge and the Daltons went way back. I went right home from the courthouse and got on the computer."

He lifted his gaze, gave her a mocking smile.

"Found plenty of coverage about the Daltons of Oklahoma City but didn't see much mention of you. Made me think you were keeping a low profile for a reason, so I dug deeper and found a petition filed with the Oklahoma County clerk's office to establish paternity of the infant referred to as Margaret 'Molly' Dalton."

The smile took a hard twist.

"So I made some calls, cuz, and discovered a woman matching your description showed up at Dalton's mama's place almost the same day as the infant. I knew the kid wasn't yours. I'd been watching you too close. So there could only be one reason why you'd take a leave of absence from your job to work as a nanny."

The mask slipped, releasing the fury behind it.

"The brat is Hope's, isn't it? My whore of a

wife had a kid by this guy Dalton, and noble, do-gooding Cousin Grace rushed to the rescue just like she always did."

"Jack…"

"Shut up! Don't even try to lie your way out of this. The kid's birth certificate was included in the paternity petition. Didn't take a genius to link her birth to the death certificate filed in the same California courthouse."

He shoved away from the table, the hate now a living thing. Grace tried not to flinch as he stalked across the room.

"She died out there," he raged. "Hope died, and you didn't even let me bury my wife."

"Jack, please. She…"

"Shut up!"

The backhand exploded against her cheek and slammed her head against the metal pole. Tasting blood, Grace fought to blink away the black spots blurring her vision.

"You're going to pay for what you did, bitch. You and Dalton."

With that implacable promise, Petrie went back to the table and picked up the rifle. Grace was still swallowing hot, coppery blood when the door banged shut and the screen door screeched behind him.

Her head swam. The whole side of her face hurt. She slumped against the metal post until she gritted her teeth and forced herself to think through the pain.

The cabin sat on a high slope that gave a commanding view of the only road in. Anyone approaching by boat would be similarly exposed. Grace couldn't wait for Petrie to pick Blake off. She wouldn't!

Breathing through her nose, she twisted to look up at the bunk above her. Its mattress was rolled up, too, revealing a crosshatch of springs hooked through the rectangular metal frame bolted to support poles.

No, wait! She blinked again, praying her still spinning head wasn't registering a blurred image. The frame wasn't bolted. With the first thrill of hope she'd felt since she'd regained consciousness, Grace saw the frame fit into Y-shaped supports.

If she could lift the frame out of the supports…

Slide the cuff up and off the pole…

She stretched out on the dank mattress and listened for any sound indicating Petrie's return, but all she could hear was the thunder of her own heart. Keeping a wary eye on the door, she rolled up on her hips and planted her feet against a corner of the frame above her.

It didn't budge. Jaw clenched, she pushed again. There was a squeak of rusted metal, an infinitesimal shift. Grunting with effort, Grace applied more leverage and got the frame half out of the support. The cry of the screen door made her drop it and her legs instantly.

"Had to set up a few electronic trip wires," Petrie informed her when he entered. With brutal nonchalance as he dropped some kind of a battery-operated device on the table. "We don't want your husband to burst in on us unannounced, do we? Now all we have to do is wait."

Neither Grace nor Petrie had any way of knowing his electronic sensors would work against, not for, him.

She lay in stark terror for what felt like hours, alternately praying the black box wouldn't beep and praying it would signal the arrival of an entire SWAT team. When the box finally gave two loud, distinctive pings, her heart stopped dead in her chest.

Then everything seemed to happen in fast-forward. She didn't have time to think, barely had time to choke back a sob before Petrie grabbed the rifle and charged for the door. He left it open, giving her a partial view of his body shielded by one of the concrete block columns and the rifle nested snug against his shoulder. Frantic, she rolled onto her hips and jabbed her feet at the upper bunk's metal frame.

"That you, Dalton?"

The answer came just as Grace got the corner of the frame off the supports.

"It's me. I'm coming in."

The frame dropped at a sharp angle, its rusted edges almost slicing into her face. She rolled out from under them just in time and somehow managed to keep the handcuffs from making more than a brief rattle. Petrie didn't hear it, thank

God. His focus and his aim were both on the figure climbing the slope.

"Walk slow," he bellowed, "and keep your hands in the air."

Panting with fear and desperation, Grace eased off the bunk and then slid the cuff up, off the metal pole. The steel bracelet dangled from her other wrist as she searched frantically for a weapon, any kind of a weapon. The only thing within reach that wasn't nailed down were the fishing rods. If nothing else, she could slash and whip one of them. She scooped one up and was frantically trying to disengage it from the others when Petrie bellowed a warning.

"You can stop there."

Grace could see Blake now, unarmed, more than close enough for a high-powered hunting rifle to drill a hole through his heart.

"I got a score to settle with you, Dalton. I'm going to do it slow, though. I think maybe I'll put the first bullet in your kneecap."

"You can put a bullet wherever the hell you want, Petrie. Just let my wife go first."

"I don't think so, pal. She's got as much to answer for as..."

Two loud pings stopped him cold. Instinctively, he tilted his head an inch or two toward the intrusion detection device still sitting on the table. Grace knew that was all the break she'd get. She lunged through the open door, arm raised, fist wrapped around the rubber handle of the fishing pole, and lashed into Petrie's face with everything she had.

"Sunuvabitch!"

He flung out an arm, caught her broadside and sent her crashing. She slammed into the hard ground and caught only a brief glimpse of Blake hurtling past her in a flying tackle. She was rolling onto a hip, dazed and shaken, when a second figure burst out of the brush on the opposite side of the clearing and raced for the cabin.

Alex pounded past her onto the porch. Blake didn't need his brother's help, Grace saw as she staggered to her feet. He had Petrie on his back, straddling his hips while he smashed a fist into his face with lethal precision.

A dazed corner of her mind wondered how a corporate attorney could take down a trained cop. Then she remembered the tales Delilah had recounted about her sons' rough-and-tumble childhood in Oklahoma's oil fields and saw firsthand the rage her husband put into every blow.

Finally, Alex had to intervene. "That's enough. Jesus, you'll kill him."

He caught his brother's arm and hauled him off a now almost unrecognizable Petrie.

"He's… He's got another gun." Still winded from her fall, Grace steadied herself with a hand on the cinder blocks and gasped for breath. "In his waistband, at his back."

Blake rolled the man over and took possession of the pistol. Thumbing the safety with practiced ease, he passed it to his brother.

"If the bastard tries to get up, blow his head off."

Then he was beside her, his blue eyes savage when he took in the bruise she knew had flowered after Petrie's backhanded blow.

"I'm okay," she said before he could spin around

and add to the punishment he'd already inflicted. "Just winded…and scared."

"Me, too," he admitted hoarsely, cupping her unbruised cheek with a bloody palm. "God, I was terrified we wouldn't get here in time."

She didn't ask how he'd found her. The details didn't matter now. All she needed, all she wanted at that moment was to lean into his hard, welcoming body.

He held her off and looked down at her with grim intent. "I never told you I love you. That ripped at me the whole time we tracked you."

She managed a shaky smile. "Well, now that you're here…"

"I love you, Grace. I'm sorry it took almost losing you to make me realize how much. Maybe someday you'll forgive me for that."

"I will. I do. And you have to forgive me for almost letting my promise to Anne blind me to the promise I made you."

"I will. I do."

She went up on tiptoe and brushed her mouth over his—very carefully.

"I love you, too." She put her whole heart into

the simple words. "So much I can't remember what it was like to *not* love you. Now take me home so we can clean our scrapes and bruises and start our marriage over."

Epilogue

Delilah insisted on celebrating her granddaughter's first birthday with her usual flamboyance and flair. As one of the Oklahoma City Zoo's most generous benefactors, she chose that as the venue for the momentous event and marshaled her entire staff to prepare for it.

Her social secretary drew up the guest list, which included fifty of Delilah's closest friends— all potential donors for a new exotic bird aviary— as well as every child enrolled in the Oklahoma City Special Olympics.

Louis, her majestic butler, came up with the design for the colorful invitations. They featured a talking parrot who squawked out the delights in store.

Her chef baked the six-layer jungle-themed main cake himself but graciously allowed a caterer to handle the rest of the menu items.

Naturally, Delilah also marshaled her daughters-in-law for party duty. She brushed aside the fact that Julie had turned over crop-dusting operations to her partners and the two additional pilots they'd brought on board. Julie's current responsibilities as director of flight operations for Dalton International kept her twice as busy, but Delilah blithely announced she could take the necessary time off to help with this once-in-a-lifetime event, as could Blake and Alex. Grace, who had delayed going back to teaching for a year or two, was totally immersed in the early preparations and event itself.

When the big day arrived, Delilah assigned her daughters-in-law the job of welcoming invitees and handing out goody bags crammed with beak-billed ball caps, macaw whistles, parrot sunglasses and canary-shaped marshmallow bars. Alex she put to work matching golf carts with drivers for kids who had difficulty walking. Blake had been tasked to assist a Special Olympics coordinator organize games suitable for children with varying disabilities. Bow-legged Dusty Jones and various volunteers from DI manned the lemonade, popcorn and cotton-candy stands set up throughout the zoo.

Even Molly participated. Spouting gibberish only she could understand, she played pat-a-cake with anyone who would reciprocate and toddled on wobbly legs after brightly colored beach balls in the infants' roller-derby. She also locked her arms around several other kids and refused to let go.

"She's at the hugging and kissing stage," Grace explained apologetically as she disentangled her daughter from a red-faced three year old. "C'mon, Mol-i-gans, it's time to blow out your candle and cut the cake."

Molly came into her arms with a smile so joyous that Grace's chest squeezed. She could see more of her cousin in the baby now. Not the frightened, cowed woman Hope had become, but the happy, laughing girl Grace had skated and played hop scotch and made mud pies with. Tears stung as she stood for a moment amid the bird calls and colorful chaos, nuzzling the squirming infant.

Oh, Hope! She's so bright and beautiful. Just like you.

Then she spotted her husband weaving his way through the crowd. A grinning boy in leg braces rode on his shoulders, waving energetically with one hand while he kept a death grip on Blake's hair with the other. When they reached his mother, Blake dipped so she could lift her son down and stopped to exchange a few words with her.

Grace's chest went tight again. Could her life be any fuller? Could her heart? This kind, thoughtful, incredibly sexy man filled every nook and cranny of her being. He and Molly and the child just beginning to take shape in her belly. She'd never dreamed she could feel such all-consuming happiness—and such a sharp stab of panic as when Molly gave a joyous cry and all but launched herself from her arms.

"Dada!"

Experience had taught Grace to keep a secure lock on the chubby little legs, thank goodness. Laughing in delight at her neat trick, Molly hung upside down until Blake righted her.

"Think you're pretty smart, don't you?"

"Smart," she echoed from the nest of his arms, adding to her growing vocabulary of one-syllable words. "Molly smart."

"Yes, you are. Very smart."

He angled her against his chest and slipped his free arm around Grace's waist. "Mother texted me with orders to convene for the cake cutting."

"Me, too. Guess we'd better comply."

They met Alex and Julie where the paths to the aviary converged.

"Un-ca!"

Molly reached out imperious arms and was duly passed to her uncle. While he and Blake led the way to the tables groaning with cake and other goodies, Julie fell into step with Grace.

"When are you going to tell Delilah you're pregnant?"

"We were thinking after the party might be a

good time. She'll be too pooped to rush over to our house and start redecorating the nursery."

"Ha! Don't bet on it." The auburn-haired pilot hesitated for a moment, a rueful smile in her unusual eyes. "Listen, sweetie, I don't want to steal your thunder, but… Well…"

"Julie!" Grace swung around. "You, too?"

"Me, too, unless the stick I peed on this morning is defective."

"Omigod! This is wonderful! Delilah will have to divide her energy between the two of us!"

Julie burst out laughing. "I thought that advantage might occur to you. It certainly did to me."

They waited to spring the news on their mother-in-law until after the last of the guests had left. The family sat amid the party debris to catch their breath before pitching in to help the cleanup crews. Molly was sound asleep in the stroller parked between Grace and Blake. Alex sprawled long-limbed and loose at a picnic table with Julie beside him. Delilah drooped in a folding chair, sighing in ecstasy when Dusty pushed his battered straw Stetson back on his head and began to knead her shoulders. Weariness etched lines in her face but she essayed a smile as she surveyed the deflating balloons and animal-shaped confetti littering the scene.

"The party went well, don't you think?"

"I'd say so," Blake agreed lazily. "How much in pledges did you strong-arm out of your friends?"

His mother's smile turned smug. "Just over a hundred thousand. They could hardly balk when I promised my sons would match them dollar for dollar."

Neither son so much as blinked at this blithe reach into their pockets.

"Half goes to Special Olympics," Delilah continued, wincing a bit as Dusty's gnarled fingers found a knot. "The other half should cover the new exotic bird aviary. The Zoo Director was thrilled at the news."

Grace and Julie exchanged glances, then both women telegraphed unspoken signals to their husbands. Blake took the cue first.

"Grace and I have some exciting news, too."

Delilah shot upright and skewered Grace with keen blue eyes. "I knew it! You're pregnant!"

Chortling, she twisted to give Dusty a triumphant grin. "Didn't I tell you that wasn't the flu that had her tossing up her breakfast last week?"

"Yep, you did."

The matriarch faced front again and trained her laser eyes on Julie. "What about you? I figure there was a reason you quit working with chemicals six months ago. You and Alex trying for a baby?"

"Not trying," Julie admitted. "Having."

"Whooeee!"

Dusty's gleeful shout made Molly jerk in her stroller. Startled, she puckered her lips and blinked once or twice, then settled back into sleep while the crop duster danced a quick jig.

"I'm gonna be a three-time grandpa. Not honorary, either," he added when he spun to a stop. Under his bushy white brows, his glance turned to Delilah. "Guess this would be a good time we tell 'em our news, Del."

"Guess so."

The sapphire bangle she always wore winked on her wrist as she reached for the thorny palm he held out to her. She didn't have to go into detail, though. Both sons and daughters-in-law were already on their feet.

"About time you made an honest man out of him," Alex said with a wide grin as he pulled her out of her chair and wrapped her in a fierce hug. He yielded his place to Blake, who echoed his brother's sentiments.

"We've been wondering when you two were going to come out of the closet. Literally."

To the amazement of all present, Delilah blushed a rosy red. Dusty merely beamed while Julie enveloped his bride-to-be in another hug.

"I'm so happy for you." Her laughing glance went to her former partner. "And if anyone can keep you out of the casinos, you old reprobate, it's Delilah."

Grace waited her turn, her heart so full it was almost a physical ache. She'd promised during Hope's last, anguished hours to deliver Molly to her father and make sure she was loved.

She is, Hope. So very loved.

So was Grace. She felt its embrace when she walked into Delilah's arms and met her husband's eyes over his mother's shoulder.

Whatever happened, whatever came in the years ahead, this was one promise she and Blake would always keep.

* * * * *